Lake View
and
Rocky Peaks

R. D. Zachman

ACKNOWLEDGEMENTS

The author recognizes and is thankful for various suggestions and help from his wife, Mary. He also acknowledges the interest and inquiries from others of his family while he was working on this project.

However, the author takes full responsibility for any errors in format, grammar, editing or other flaws that might occur on the pages of this book.

Dedication

I dedicate this book, in part (posthumously) to my former college English Professor, Dr. Richard Snyder. Professor Snyder recommended that I continue reading novels after I had enjoyed taking his course, 'The Modern American Novel', at Ashland College in the late 1950's. I found his advice very worthwhile.

I also dedicate this, my first novel, to Author Craig Johnson. I was fortunate enough to have a conversation with Author Johnson at one of his book signings a few years ago. At that time, he gave me suggestions and personal encouragement on how to begin the writing process

RDZ

Lake View and Rocky Peaks

Dr. Victor Moritz, age 43, walked confidently along the path leading to the research building adjacent to the Lake View Medical Center Hospital. His six foot-two fit and muscular body moved smoothly in a traditional fitted dress suit and tie. His face was lean and sharp, with penetrating blue eyes, focused directly ahead. There was a slight frown on his forehead suggesting serious thought about some issue.

Today he would face the Medical Center's 'Patient Care and Research Ethics Committee' to present his logic and scientific rationale in seeking approval by the Committee for his clinical study treatment protocol. This clinical study was for treating prostate cancer bone metastases. His research was sound, and he already had approval for a clinical study trial from the U.S. Food and Drug Administration (FDA). However, the Medical Center's Committee must also approve his proposal before allowing use of the treatment in patients at their Hospital. Dr. Moritz was hopeful for approval because other therapies tried on these very ill patients to date had failed to halt the cancer's progression or improve the patient's condition.

Dr. Moritz was of German and Swiss descent.

His grandfather, Karl, came from Germany to America in 1887 at the age of 25. Karl had gained some experience as an entry draftsman after his honor student performance gave him a year of free schooling in Arts and Language at the secondary school in Leipzig. After arriving in America, the family settled in Ohio. Karl eventually wed Victor's grandmother, Catherine Baer, whose family had come to America in 1861, just before the outbreak of the Civil War. Karl and Catherine settled on a 45 acre farm in central Ohio. Karl became a stone cutter and was commissioned to cut for several church foundations, as well as many houses in the area. George Moritz, Victor's father, was born in 1904. In 1933, he married Garnet Schneeberger, whose ancestors arrived in America in the 1850's from Switzerland.

Moritz recalled these roots often when considering his own opportunities of education. He felt his family had influenced his drive to do quality work, his pursuit of independence and self-respect. His ancestral tree consisted of a stone cutter, farmers, a shoe cobbler, dedicated stay at home housewives ,and a gasoline station proprietor, none with a college degree. He took pride in all the written items he had seen stored in old trunks from their days, and had listened intently to the conversations with his parents and grandparents that had told of their family history and values. They had strived to do the best at any work they undertook, practiced honesty, fair exchange, and interacted with fellow humans with moral respect.

***

Now however, Moritz's thoughts turned to the events leading to the present situation of the Committee meeting. After graduation from Medical School and then completing training programs in adult Medicine and Oncology, he joined the Faculty at The Ohio State School of Medicine. There, he became a respected member of the Medical School, acknowledged for his excellence in patient care, progress in research, and data based objective teaching.

At one of the outlying regional Hospitals where Victor Moritz had been invited to give a lecture to the medical staff, he met Rachel, who in two years, became his wife. When they met, Rachel was that regional Hospital's administrative assistant for their Faculty's required Continuing Medical Education program. With their first meeting, Victor and Rachel liked each other. Then, over the next two years, Victor and Rachel saw and spent time together as often as living 80 miles apart could be arranged. They experienced dinner together, a show, picnic, or weekends of outdoor activity as often as possible. Rachel then moved to Columbus, secured a job with the city library, and they married. Victor's professional activities were going well and her work was rewarding. They shared, communicated, and were honest and respectful with each other. To put it simply, they were in love and best friends.

The tragedy occurred nearly 3 years after their marriage. Rachel's family still lived back in the community where Victor had met her. Since her parents were aging, but trying to manage living in their own home, Rachel returned to visit them every two weeks. One evening on the road, fog and black ice caused the despicable accident that took her life, as well as the couple in the horse drawn Amish buggy that suddenly appeared over an unanticipated rise in the road that was undergoing new construction.

Victor arrived at the Hospital as soon as possible and in time to speak to Rachel, in her near comatose and dying condition. He was able to feel a weak hand squeeze in response to his holding her hand for a brief few seconds before she coded and became unresponsive to all resuscitative efforts by the Hospital staff. Although his grieving and memories of Rachel had become less frequent over the years, this past love lost would always be remembered. It came crashing through his thoughts at unpredictable times. One of those times was suddenly now. Dr. Victor Moritz abruptly stopped walking as this memory surfaced. Finally, after a couple of deep breaths, he resumed walking toward his laboratory in the research building.

***

 Moritz thought this Committee he would face today could go either way with their response to his treatment study request. He had sent them several documents which described the method and its mechanism of action, including copies of his recent scientific publications. He had also sent a review describing why this therapy was being tested. This included the facts that bone metastases from prostate cancer had a poor response to other treatments, its aggressive and invasive progression, and descriptions of the end stage conditions of the patients awaiting a treatment. He had even sent a copy of a prospective patient's own note to the Committee, which pleaded with them for a favorable response to Moritz's request to start a clinical study trial using his proposed treatment.

Moritz was counting on strong support from at least two of the Committee members, but also knew that 2 of the 5 were Faculty that had, for a few years in fact, been critical of his ideas. They held this view in spite of the fact that many peer researchers at other institutions were supportive of Moritz's findings, and urged him to go forward with a clinical study. These 2 Committee members were also vocal in their accusing Moritz of being too self-centered and focused mainly on his own program, rather than being more of a team player for some of their own priorities.

As the research building came into view, Dr. Moritz's thoughts went from this afternoon's meeting to remembering his arrival at the Lake View Medical Center. He had lost Rachel when he was 38 years old, had stayed at Ohio State for 1 more year, then moved to Lake View. Part of the move was because of the bitter memory of the fateful event. However, other factors also influenced his decision.

***

Lake View's facility was a Regional Referral Center for complex cancer patient diagnosis and treatment. As importantly, he was also recruited vigorously by the Lake View Hospital and Medical School. They had a newly established endowment for an Oncology physician - scientist and wanted to fill the position with someone not already on their Faculty. Victor Moritz's research background, his clinical work, and his expert teaching were praised by those that wrote Lake View in support of his application. He had also been advised by a trusted friend and mentor to go for an interview and consider seriously this position. The job offer was finalized and he moved to Lake View.

Moritz's arrival at the Lake View Medical Center was a memorable event that he experiences every day going to work. The buildings of the main Hospital, research center, library, and housing for patients' families, lay on well landscaped clean grounds contoured to blend into the surrounding lake and lush woods. The structures and grounds could be viewed as an island of hope for seriously ill patients. The maintenance and support buildings fit easily into the landscape as well.

The Center was clearly separated from the surrounding community and housing developments, which were some seven miles to the East. When Moritz had come for the interview, he was also immediately impressed by those Faculty he met already working at the Center. They were enthusiastic and dedicated to bringing their best effort to their work. All seemed to be striving to do some part in bringing to the Lake View Medical Center a significant reputation as a cancer treatment Hospital, as well as having a number of research and teaching accomplishments.

2

Dr. Moritz's research laboratory was on the second of four floors in the Research Building, next to the Hospital complex. His purpose this morning was to meet with members of his research group to see if the experiments of yesterday could add anything new to the information he was going to present to the Committee that afternoon.

Dr. Li Chen was in her 3rd year of a postdoctoral Fellowship in Oncology. As a PhD Biochemistry graduate of the University of Washington in Seattle, she had joined Dr. Moritz's program at Lake View. Li was not married and was in her early 30's at the time. She lived close to the complex in a single bedroom apartment in a building the Center had built specifically for employees that did not want to live further away in other more traditional communities. She had wanted to avoid the necessity of commuting. Dr. Chen also was not interested in much social life, and often spent more than a regular 8 hour day contributing to the progress of Moritz's research program.

Moritz's laboratory and research activities were financially supported by several sources. A minor portion came from the Lake View Medical Center. However, Moritz's main sources of grant money were from pharmaceutical companies, the National

Cancer Institute (NCI) and the American Cancer Society (ACS). Additionally, a smaller, but meaningful amount, was gifted by patients and families who previously had been treated at the Hospital.

The laboratory was of a modest space, was short on décor and furnishings, but had state of the art scientific technology and equipment. Dr. Chen had a small private office, with windows, that was shared with Dr. Moritz when he was not at his clinic office in the Hospital. Another member of the research group was a Graduate Student working on his PhD degree. Finally, one part time 4th year Medical Student worked there 20 hours per week. Each of these two had a desk cubicle at the end of a laboratory bench counter.

There was easy access to other research rooms that were used and shared by persons of all the laboratory programs on the 2nd floor. These areas had specialized complex instruments and minus 70 degrees freezer space for storing biological samples and chemicals that required temperatures much below zero. There were also walk in refrigerated rooms for procedures requiring cold, but not freezer conditions, such as cell preparations. Isolation rooms, where sterile procedures could be performed, were also available. Supporting facilities such as experimental animal quarters, irradiation exposure rooms, major data technology, and others, were on different floors of the building.

Dr. Chen was expecting Dr. Moritz and they welcomed each other with a handshake. Li had her long black hair up in a bun as usual, and her clean lab coat fit neatly. There was no tea, coffee, or snacks in the lab or office, as food consumption was allowed only in the break rooms on each floor. This was necessary because of possible accidental contamination of food with radioisotopes, traces of toxic chemicals, or other biological hazards.

Li's science report to Moritz was quite important, and was short and to the point. She confirmed that all of the materials needed to go forward with a clinical study were on hand, and ready to be combined and used.

This was very good news to Dr. Moritz. During the past several months, the treatment they have developed had significantly cured bone metastases from prostate cancer in laboratory animals. Now it was time to do a clinical study, using this newly developed treatment. He was hoping to be able to begin such a clinical study within 2-4 weeks, pending approval by the Patient Care and Research Ethics Committee. Study patients would be those whose prostate cancer cells were now causing their bone cancer which had not responded to any other conventional treatment protocols. These patients were classified as terminal, destined to die from their illness within a few months.

So, the laboratory materials were ready. However, Moritz told Dr. Chen not to start the process of combining the separate agents into the final treatment complex until he had received absolute final approval from the Committee.

The Graduate Student, Mark and Medical Student, Charlie had come into the laboratory by this time. After greetings, there was some small talk until they were asked to come into the office with Chen and Moritz. Each of them presented a 5-10 minute briefing of their latest experiments and plans for the week, and then returned to the laboratory and began their work.

***

Dr. Chen then gave Moritz a look indicating she had something more to say to him. She got up and closed the office door.

"I had some visitors earlier this morning that you need to know about": she said, with a worried look on her expression as she changed position in her chair.

Moritz said: "I hope it was not someone I think it

might have been."

Chen said: "Yes, two members of the Committee, Dr. Green and Dr. Smith, were waiting at the door when I came to work at 7:00 AM this morning. They asked to come in, and of course I said 'yes' as I was coming in anyway. When I had changed into my lab coat, they asked if we might sit down for a few minutes to talk."

Moritz said, frowning: "You were at their mercy, it doesn't sound good."

Li continued: "They started with a brief review of what they understood about our work, including the potential value of our approach. However, they insinuated there must have been some negative results or bad outcomes with our research, and asked to see some of that data. I told them that all trials with our new antibody and transporter method in animal experiments were positive and that every experimental control used in our studies was valid. I told them that our work had been favorably reviewed by several researchers at other Cancer Research Centers. These two then tried to distort my answers and trick me by their multiple questions, talking at the same time, scoffing and raising their voices to intimidate me."

Li now raised her voice for emphasis: "They

accused us of covering up negative data. They said they had heard rumors from my graduate school Professor that I had falsified data for my Thesis, which is totally not true."

At this point while speaking with Moritz, Li was nearly in tears and literally shaking in her chair.

Moritz reached out and gently, but firmly, steadied her arm and said: "I'm so sorry about this happening. I wish I would have arrived here earlier this morning. But if you can, Li, please go on if there is more."

Li steadied herself and continued: "They also tried to bribe me. The first attempt was with bonus dollars from what they called 'the Science Division's Contingency Fund' if I would give them some statement saying 'I was suspicious of some of the claims you made when reporting our results.' Next they said they could get me promoted to a Senior Scientist Position with a 5 year appointment guaranteed, instead of my having to wait another year for the promotion that is generally required for the usual Postdoctoral tract. I only would have to state, in writing, that I knew of negative results and had knowledge of altered experimental outcomes to make the data always favorable to our hypothesis and our laboratory's goals." Li was now sobbing out of control.

"After I refused to do such unreal things, they finally left the lab."

Dr. Victor Moritz was stunned. He briefly felt helpless and angry, but shook it off. He offered Li some tissues from the box on her desk. Then he sat back and waited until she had become calm again.

Moritz finally said: "Li, let me say once more how sorry I am that these parasites came after you. Let's try to think about what options we have, what should we do about this attack? It would not help our project and efforts towards finally getting a clinical study in patients if we react too aggressively at this time. This would only make these specific Committee members all the more opposed to our efforts."

"I could go to Lake View's Scientific Director, tell him what happened and request some action against these two Professors. However, given the fact these two just happen to hold considerable influence over some valued financial donors to our Center, and are close to the President of Lake View, the Director's hands might be tied. Since no one else was witness to the harassment, it would be your word against those two Faculty members of the Center. I am afraid you, at the Post-doctoral level, would not get as much consideration as these long time Professors of this institution. I know it should be equal consideration, but I don't think it would be likely."

"For now, Li, I ask you to keep this between us. Please do not even share any of this with the others in our laboratory, nor anyone else. I will, at the Committee meeting today, go ahead with my presentation and answer their scientific queries as scheduled. However, I will hold in reserve this despicable act that happened to you this morning."

"Li, I know this has been terribly hard on you. I promise you, this issue will surface at a later time and hopefully these two will then have to atone for it."

3

The conference room for the meeting was off a hallway of the science library. The location was a multi- purpose room with moveable tables. The tables set up for today were in a half circle with chairs for 10-12 people, where all could easily face the front of the room. The open end of the arrangement had a small desk, with computer controls for any usual needed visual aids for presentations. Available at the desk was a straight backed rolling chair for the one giving a lecture to use while preparing or presenting their material.

Dr. Moritz arrived 30 minutes earlier than the 2:00 PM scheduled meeting time. He wanted to load and review quickly his power point material. He also set out for each Committee member an outline of his presentation. This handout guide had ample room for those listening to write notes regarding his presentation, or thoughts they wanted to explore in a discussion.

The Committee members started arriving and getting settled a few minutes before 2:00 PM. Each greeted Victor Moritz with a word or brief glance. The mood of this meeting seemed already fairly tense and serious. The Patient Care and Research Ethics Committee consisted of five members. One was a lay person named Rob Olson.

Two were cancer basic science research Faculty, Jerry Smith, PhD. and Phil Johnson, PhD, MD. There were also two Oncology Clinical Faculty, David Green, PhD, MD. and Rebecca Lopez, MD.

Rob Olson's family had recently experienced a cancer caused death of his sister, Sandy, despite all the state of the art methods used in her treatment at the Lake View Hospital. Rob was born into a poor, wrong side of the tracks family in a community 45 miles from the Center. However, with his old pick-up truck and experiences gained at several part time construction jobs, Rob put together what he had learned, and then developed his own trucking and construction business. His business now had contracts for work throughout a three county area that was in and adjacent to the county in which the Valley View Center was located. Rob Olson's honesty, hard work, respect for others and their property, fairness in pay or trade for services, and thinking the best of others were some of the factors that had led the Director of Science at Lake View to select him as the lay person for this Committee. In addition, it was generally known that Rob was a compassionate person, doing some volunteer work and charitable activities on weekends or when his business was slow.

Dr. Jerry Smith earned his PhD. in Oncology research from UCLA and had been at Lake View for 5 years. He was working on some of the basic science of the causes and the development of breast cancer.   Victor Moritz knew of Jerry's research efforts and they had discussed each other's projects several times in the past. Moritz's concern with Jerry at this time was the feeling that, for some reason, Jerry was always in support of Dr. David Green when it came to Faculty discussions, dispersing funds for research within the Center, and other situations. Jerry was also on several of Dr. Green's Committees throughout the Center.

Dr. Phil Johnson earned his MD. and PhD. in cancer biology at the MD Anderson School of Medicine in Dallas, TX. He had been at the Lake View Center since its opening now 12 years ago. Johnson had developed a new drug for use in treating a type of children's cancer. A patent for the discovery had helped the research funds of the Center significantly since that time. Recently, it was suspected that Johnson might be considering a move to another Center that was offering him a job as Chairman of an entire Cancer Biology Program in the West. He was known for his knack of looking at a basic research project, not only his own, but also of others, and pointing out paths to facilitate translational medicine. This was when the observations of the laboratory are efficiently translated into patient use in clinical medicine at the bedside. To Dr. Johnson, objective judgements based on facts were a virtue to wear openly.

Dr. David Green received his PhD, MD. degrees at Penn State and did his Residency and subspecialty training in adult Oncology at Columbia University. His age was in the 50's, and he sat on several important policy and financial Committees in the Center. He therefore had the ear of several of the Administrators at the Center and some influence over certain Faculty members. The Committee reviewing Moritz's project was only a short term assignment for all members. The selection had been done by the Director of Science, the Chief of the Clinical Medical Staff, and the Director of Human Resources. Green was chairman of this Committee reviewing Moritz's clinical study protocol.

The fifth member of the Committee was Dr. Rebecca Lopez. Dr. Lopez earned her MD. at the J. Hillis Miller Health Center in Gainesville, FL. and then did her Residency and Fellowship in Oncology, with an emphasis on women's cancer, in San Diego. She was successful in being hired to fill an opening at Lake View upon completion of her training, now six years ago. Dr. Lopez had a reputation for an excellent bedside manner, and explaining to her patients their situation with straightforward and understandable conversation. She was very compassionate with patients, their family and support persons. She had dark eyes, long black hair that was up in a bun while in the Hospital, and a beautiful oval face topping a five foot nine slim figure.

Everyone found a comfortable seat with a good view of where Dr. Moritz would stand, present his material and respond to questions.

***

Dr. Green spoke: "The purpose of this meeting is to have Dr. Moritz present a proposal to use his new anti-cancer therapy on a series of terminal patients with prostate cancer that has metastasized to bone. He is here to clarify his proposal and convince our Patient Care and Research Ethics Committee of its merit, enough to warrant allowing him to do a clinical study using his approach in our Center. This decision will be based, at least in part, on the reliability and objective assessment of the data and experimental work leading to his unique approach.   It also requires the demonstration of a logical rationale for the selection of patients, and the risk/benefits ratio weighed against alternative approaches. Any questions?"

No one spoke up.

Green said: "OK, Dr. Moritz, you have our attention."

***

Victor Moritz stood. He suppressed the anger he had for Green and Smith at this time, cleared his throat, and began speaking: "I thank the Center and this Committee's members for this opportunity. I will briefly give an overall summary of our project and then allow plenty of time for you to ask me questions and express your concerns that we might discuss or clarify further. Then I will present more in depth experimental results that any of the Committee would like to hear about."

Moritz continued: "The prostate is the most frequent organ in which cancer arises in males, an accounts for over 26,000 deaths per year in America. There are several opinions presently about how to most accurately diagnose significant prostate cancer and what early treatment to use. What is very apparent, however, is that most prostate cancer deaths occur because of prostate cancer cells metastasizing, that is, leaving the prostate and invading other tissue. These metastases most commonly occur to bone, although other organs are sometimes invaded as well."

"As with many cancers, involvement and failure of organs invaded at these secondary sites of cancer are typically harder to identify and treat. These aggressive metastatic cells often set about their destructive activity in small vascular 'niches' that many times are not accessible with our usual therapeutic approaches of treatment. As importantly, sometimes the identifying markers on metastatic cells is altered so that many therapeutic attempts fail to target these cells and thus do not destroy them."

"Our project is focused on prostate cancer patients that have metastatic bone disease which has not responded to other conventional therapeutic attempts. These patients are classified as terminal, patients untreatable with standard approaches and are likely to die within a few months."

Dr. Moritz paused, took a sip of water and continued: "We have taken samples of metastatic prostate cells in bone and have identified a new, unusual, and very specific marker, or Antigen, on these cells' surface. This marker is different than the commonly used Antigen marker to identify a prostate cell, the 'Prostate Specific Antigen' (PSA). We call our discovery Antigen X."

"We have then been successful in producing a protein molecule, Antibody Y, which binds to Antigen X on the metastatic cancer cell. Our research also has learned how to facilitate delivery of that specific Antibody Y to metastatic prostate cancer cells that are thriving yet in the very small vascular niches of the invaded bone. We place this new Antibody Y on the surface of a Nanosphere. A Nanosphere, as most of you know, is a very small particle about one-two hundredths the size of a red blood cell. These particles can very easily circulate and enter the vascular niches, where the cancer cells that escaped routine therapeutic approaches, are now growing. These metastatic cells are continuing to produce more invasive cancer cells which then kill and destroy the normal cell content of the bone."

Moritz continued: "Our newly produced Antibody Y facilitates the Nanosphere binding specifically to Antigen X on these malignant cells, and leaves normal cells untouched. After this specific binding to the metastatic prostate cancer cell in bone is accomplished, another event takes place."

"The Nanospheres we use will also contain an anti-DNA molecule that inhibits cell growth and reproduction. This is accomplished through being incorporated into the malignant cell's DNA genetic material. Hence, those cells undergo cell death. So, our treatment technique is the use of a Nanosphere Complex, which involves arrival to a specific target, binding to the target and then destruction of those malignant cells. Previously, the location of the cancer cells in a small vascular niche and no unique surface markers identified, made the cancer cell unaffected by many approaches previously attempted."

"This specific binding and cell killing effectiveness of our Nanosphere Complex has been evaluated in killing metastatic prostate cancer cells in our laboratory. We have demonstrated this in cells isolated from bone cultures which contained prostate cancer cell invasion. The approach is also effective _in vivo_ in mice in our laboratory, and recently confirmed in the primate by experiments carried out at a well- known Primate Center in Northwest America."

"The FDA and National Cancer Institute(NCI) human subjects committees have reviewed our data and have approved our Nanosphere Complex for a trial in humans, pending review and approval by this 'on site' Committee, which we would appreciate very much."

Moritz took a deep breath and said: "That is the crux of our project. I will try to answer questions that you might have. I also can present specific data of proof that I have, or data which you would like to review for clarification. Thank you for your attention."

Dr. Green replied: "Thank you Dr. Moritz. I agree that the meeting should now focus on any questions members of this Committee might have."

***

Dr. Jerry Smith was the first to speak up: "Victor, I am concerned about the lack of originality here and your inexperience with Nanospheres. It is already known that such technology is being used in other cancer therapy. How can we be sure your 'Nanosphere Complex' is valid? Why should our Committee accept your approach as being worthy of this next big step, using it on human patients?"

Moritz thought for a moment and then said: "Yes, I know Nano-technology has now been around for several years and that the use in medicine is expanding, and certainly one of the areas is in cancer biology. Also, admittedly, I am not an expert in Nanospheres."

"However, our research and proposed clinical study is on solid ground. We are obtaining our Nanospheres from a well- known Nano-Technology facility in Tokyo. The structure is a sphere that contains both a central core for the anti- DNA molecule, and a specific surface to which Antibody Y is easily attached. Uniquely, upon attachment of the Nanosphere carried Antibody Y to the Antigen X on the metastatic cancer cell, the outer layer of the Nanosphere we are using forms a channel that connects the inside of the Nanosphere to the inside of the cancer cell. This allows the cancer killing growth anti-DNA contents of our Nanosphere Complex to enter the cancer cell and inhibits that cell's further growth, replication, and bone destruction."

"Another property of these spheres we are using includes an outer layer that prevents breakdown in the surroundings of normal cell environments, so normal cells are not affected. Our Nanospheres do not attach to, nor break down normal cells. Jerry, our clinical proposal is worth trying."

Jerry Smith tilted his head side to side, shrugged his shoulders and then said: "I also have some concerns about the statistics you used to arrive at some of your conclusions. I might bring this up later." Then he sat back in his chair, looking at Dr. David Green, with a facial expression that said, 'How did I do'?

Phil Johnson raised his hand and spoke up: "I have read several of Victor's publications on this project as well as the materials he gave us 2 weeks ago. There is a definitive answer to your second concern, Jerry. All of the published material and the other material I just spoke of in Dr. Moritz's handouts, have clearly been reviewed by the statisticians of Lake View, which are excellent. In addition, a separate statistical group from outside our Center has reviewed the material with the same conclusions. They are all clear in their support of the rationale and validity of Victor's statistical approaches to the material. They, to a person, state their confidence in the interpretation of his results."

Dr. Johnson, wiping blond hair back from his forehead, continued: "For me, in the quest for the truth in science research, objectivity is paramount. Dr. Victor Moritz has objectively, not randomly or by emotion, assessed his basic research findings, and verified the truth where, and if, there was any ambiguous findings. He now proposes the translation of his basic research to be tested for actual clinical usefulness. 'Bench to Bedside' is what we strive for. I strongly support going forward with the next step. That is the clinical study he requests here."

Dr. David Green, with some graying hair and receding hairline at his forehead, prepared to speak next. Victor Moritz was aware that Green was well accepted by the Center's Administrative hierarchy. He held several Committee memberships, from financial to the hiring and evaluation of faculty members. Victor was therefore somewhat worried, even before Green's thoughts were verbalized. He also thought about Green's confrontation this morning with Li Chen.

"Dr. Moritz, I will accept your background work on the project, although I agree somewhat with Jerry's stated concerns. I also have some additional comments. One relates to trying to hold down the costs of medical care. I know that Nanosphere synthesis in general, is very costly. Making a very specific Nanosphere Complex that you have described, the particle being from Tokyo, seems like it will be very costly for the patient or their insurance provider. I am not sure how many insurance companies will cover the cost of a clinical trial for such a new approach that you describe."

"A related bothersome issue, in my mind, is

using such an elaborate expensive study on terminal patients. I read your plans to study these patients by expensive procedures, such as PET scans, X-Ray imaging, and frequent laboratory studies to evaluate whether the treatment approach is accomplishing anything."

"It would be much more fiscally responsible, and maybe more humane, to keep these patients on Palliative or Hospice care. In addition to their metastatic prostate cancer, they are usually an older group of men and might not even have health insurance. Our Center must try to keep down costs of picking up the tab for such an expensive project."

Dr. Green paused for a moment, then resumed: "I believe it would alert the ear of our Center's financial administrators when they learn of this project."

Moritz responded: "Dr. Green, I agree that the purchase of the basic Nanosphere particle and the preparation of the final Nanosphere Complex is expensive. Thus far, the preliminary experimental costs have been paid for by my grants from the National Cancer Institute (NCI) and the American Cancer Society (ACS). It is possible that a site in America, like in the MD Anderson Cancer Center in Dallas, could make the basic Nanosphere vehicle at a cheaper cost. This is not likely from what I understand after previously looking into this issue. In addition, we have a very excellent relationship with the Tokyo group who have supplied the Nanospheres at essentially their cost of production. Therefore, they are not making much in the bargain so far."

"Of course, if our approach is successful in killing these hidden metastatic cancer cells in bone, the Tokyo group would benefit from being recognized for their valuable contribution to the study."

"All patient costs generated by this study will be paid for through my grant awards. These are from both government and private organizations."

Moritz continued: "Regarding the patient to be treated. Each prospective patient would be in the study only after full disclosure. As best as possible, we will tell patients both the potential benefit that might occur, as well as the possibility of the approach not working, and even also of potential harm. It is up to the patient himself to enter the treatment study after being presented with the facts as we know them. No one is forcing them to enter our study."

"Dr. Green said: "I may have some other comments at another time, but in the interest of moving along, let us go on to Dr. Lopez. Rebecca, it is your turn to comment."

Dr. Lopez focused on Moritz: "Victor, a few points from my perspective. Although I have not had a basic research background, I have read some of your material, and feel that it all seems rational and sound. It was a huge break in finding that specific Antigen X on the metastatic prostate cancer cells in bone. The hard work by your lab in producing an Antibody Y is to be commended."

"As a clinical Oncologist, I see the suffering of our cancer patients on a daily basis, including the sufferings we impose on them with some of our present treatments of chemotherapy and irradiation. Although your work is targeted to a fairly small group out of the total persons suffering from cancer, I feel that you should be allowed to go forward with this clinical study."

"That being said, I agree somewhat with Dr. Green. There is some point in our profession that each must address when it is no longer in the patient's best interest to continue more and more new therapy approaches and evaluations. There comes a time when the Palliative care or Hospice approach is more appropriate. Do we put a maximum cost on our experimental care options, or age of the patient, or the expected time of survival? I just want to make sure you are considering this if you start entering patients into this clinical study protocol."

With an unnoticed, but inner feeling of relief, Dr. Moritz said: "Thank you for your comments. We are trying to approach this study being as moral in such considerations as possible."

Dr. Green then said, with a rather reluctant and condescending facial expression and body movement in his chair: "Mr. Olson, do you have anything to add to our meeting this afternoon?"

Rob Olson said: "Yes, Dr. Green, I do. Before I begin, let me thank those at Lake View that decided a lay person be invited to be a member of such an important Committee."

"I think that the discussion so far has been in terms that have been relatively clear and understood for a layman like myself. I did some serious reading of the comments written on Dr. Moritz's research by invited reviewers from outside this Center. Those reviewers were all very supportive of Dr. Moritz's background work and his forward vision for the prospective clinical study seems valid."

"I believe the question of enrollment only after the patient understands all the possibilities and options is well established and will be presented with good conscience, and hopefully also compassionately. I am thinking of my late sister, who recently died of ovarian cancer. I think she would be hoping that this proposed study would be successful and that research on the methodology and findings of this proposed study might eventually even be applied to other cancers like the ovarian cancer she had."

"I do need some clarification on the protocol, however. Dr. Moritz, can you tell me briefly, but with some detail, how actually the study will be carried out on the patient?"

Dr. Moritz, somewhat embarrassed, said: "Thank you Mr. Olson, for your question. I had sent that information to Committee members before you were asked to join. I apologize for not then remembering to send it to you before today. I will gladly give you a summary right now."

"After entry into the study, the patient will be admitted to the Hospital's outpatient clinic in the morning. First, there will be basic imaging studies to identify the extent of the bone metastases. Baseline laboratory studies on blood will also be recorded. Then, a randomly selected, coded to the patient, Nanosphere Complex dose will be given intravenously to the patient over 2 hours. When completed, the patient will remain in the clinic for 2 more hours for observation, then discharged if there are no obvious complications at the time."

"In 3 weeks, another Nanosphere Complex infusion of the same coded dose will be given after imaging and blood laboratory studies are done again. After another 3 weeks, the final Nanosphere Complex coded dose will be given after the 3rd imaging and blood laboratory studies are drawn as usual. In between the Nanoshpere Complex doses, the patient will be under observation by their own familiar Oncologist for their usual follow-up and cares."

"Any health issues arising that needs care by their own Oncologist will be recorded in the patient's clinical study record. If complications requiring hospitalization occur, we would ask that the patient be referred to Lake View to be evaluated. At 6 months, 1 year and 3 years after entry, the patients still surviving will return to clinic to receive imaging and specific blood analyses to follow the progress of their metastases. Post-mortem studies will be done at the time of a study patient's death if possible. All this data, along with that obtained at the outset of the 3 Nanosphere infusions, will be recorded in their patient data file. These confidential files of all those in the study will then be reviewed and evaluated by an unbiased NIH and ACS panel."

Rob Olson said: "Thank you Dr. Moritz. That is very helpful to me and that is all I have to ask at this time."

Subsequent to this first round of questions and discussion, Dr. Moritz was asked to review several other points of his experiments in more detail. The Committee had no serious problems with any of the data he was asked to review during this time.

**

After over two and a half hours, Dr. Green stood up and said to the Committee members and Moritz: "We have heard comments from everyone and it is getting late. We will schedule another meeting for next week. At that time, we will welcome comments from our Committee again, if they have anything to add or would like more explanation from Dr. Moritz on a particular area of his study. I will also invite the Associate Chairman of the Center's financial office to attend and discuss some of the items that arise from Dr. Moritz's proposed study and some other Lake View matters. I think if we are required to have a lay person on our Committee, I certainly can invite a financial consultant to sit in. My administrative assistant will notify you of the meeting time next week. This meeting is now adjourned."

Then Dr. David Green walked out of the room.

Most of the Committee members glanced at each other and at Victor with rather surprised looks on their faces. Slowly, they left the conference room without any more conversation.

Victor Moritz stood there alone for a few minutes. He realized there was still more effort needed to win approval of his clinical study. He also thought of how he might use the episode that occurred in his lab this morning to influence the Committee to support his study.

He then gathered his presentation materials, shut out the lights, and left the room, closing the door behind him.

4

By the time Victor Moritz left the meeting and returned to his lab, Mark and Charlie had gone to the late afternoon Pathology Seminar. However, Li Chen was still there. Li and Moritz sat and talked for several minutes. Li seemed to have recovered from the anxiety she had experienced with the unwanted Faculty intruders the first thing this morning. She listened intently as Moritz gave a brief summary of each Committee Member's questions and comments. Also, although somewhat subjective, he tried to share with her the personal attitudes of each member. He told her that he had not raised the issue of the inappropriate visit to the lab. He assured her however, that at some point in time, those Faculty would be exposed, and that the Scientific Director and other Administrative persons of the Center would be called into play on this issue. She was satisfied with all this information, and an hour later, Li and Moritz locked up and left the lab.

***

While leaving the building to walk to the parking lot, Moritz used his cell phone to dial an old friend, Otto Zellers   When the phone was answered, Moritz said: "Otto, this is Victor. I was wondering about picking up a couple sandwiches and side salads from the Hospital's Deli and coming by to talk with you for a while. Would you be OK with that?"

Otto replied: "That sounds great. I have not eaten since lunch and would enjoy a sandwich and your company. I have a bottle of wine that needs to be opened as well."

"I'll be there in about 40 minutes then." Moritz said, and clicked off his phone.

The carryout order at the Deli was quickly filled and Moritz was soon on his way. Otto Zellers lived alone in his single story, two bedroom home in a small town of about 9,000 persons, 5 miles North-West of the Lake View Medical Center. He was a retired Family Practice Physician. Dr. Zellers had practiced in the region for 40 years. He had the pleasure of having Medical Students and Residents from Lake View Hospital participate in clinical rotation experiences with patients at his office many times. He enjoyed teaching them clinical medicine. Equally fulfilling was the opportunity to just associate and interact with these motivated younger people a generation or two away from him.

After retirement, Dr. Zellers had the opportunity to continue his passion for teaching through volunteering to review and discuss cases with Medical Students twice monthly at Lake View Hospital. He had continued this interaction through 8 years after retirement, but recently had to give it up because of slowing down physically as he entered into his 80's last year. However, he was still driving his car to the local grocery store. He also enjoyed taking care of a small yard and garden, and maintaining a greenhouse of plants and flowers, which was attached to the south facing back porch of the dwelling. He did indulge in having a household cleaning service come every two weeks.

Dr. Moritz and Dr. Zellers got to know each other and become good friends through their working together in the twice monthly Medical Student clinical case review and teaching sessions. Both had similar feelings of the importance of such teaching and learning meetings. The friendship grew when they talked over coffee afterwards. Their interactions led them to discover they had similar views about many issues, so they always had something to talk about when Victor stopped by at Otto's home.

Moritz found Otto opening the bottle of wine when he arrived. After a handshake, which was their custom with greetings, there was some small talk about the weather as they got out the Deli's food onto plates Otto had already set out. Otto offered the wine cork to Victor to sniff. He did, declared it was good, and poured two glasses.

Otto was a widower now for 10 years. He was, at his age of 81, thin beyond being trim. He had a sharp nose, prominent facial bones, and surprisingly clear blue eyes that looked from behind bifocals. His gray hair was thinning back from the forehead and temples, closely cut but still lying flat except for a little brushed up slightly in front. Otto's 6 foot tall frame slightly favored his left hip on getting up from a chair and walking. Though not needing a cane as yet, it was obvious that he had pain in his upper left leg and hip areas.

Victor asked: "So, Otto, how has it been going with you since we last talked a couple weeks ago?"

Otto chuckled: "Well, Victor, about the same. Eating well enough and trying to stick to a healthy diet, except I will break training for this sandwich you brought me tonight."

He continued: "I can't complain much about my health. I figure so far I am a pretty lucky man in that regard. My left hip arthritis hurts with weight bearing and losing range of motion, but I am tolerating it to avoid surgery for now. I rarely take a pain pill. As most my age, I am on a low dose aspirin and medication to keep cholesterol in check. Otherwise no signs of serious medical issues it seems. Of course, growing older brings up some memory gaps, and I am getting weaker than I used to be, even though I get some walking and other exercise at the gym 3 times a week. I imagine the testosterone is probably dropping as I get older as well, but no hot flashes yet." Otto smiled, then took another sip of wine and began to eat the food Victor had brought and they were sharing.

He then said: "I am keeping up my interest in following sports in the paper and on TV. The house and garden work is always around. I still like to spend a couple hours a day reading, and once every two weeks I join a friendly card game with the guys. Recently the County Medical Society asked me to write an article summarizing some of my medical case experiences, and some thoughts of how medical care has changed over the past 40 years. They also wanted to hear something about my assessment of the Medical Student review sessions we had been doing. Were they useful as a teaching tool, had they been ethical and confidential? They asked me to speculate on whether the Center should allow such discussions to continue in this climate of increased patient privacy efforts that are expected during the medical education process. When I get to that part of the article, I will be contacting you to share some opinions on the question."

* * *

"Victor, now tell me about your day. I know you were presenting to Green's Committee."

Moritz finished the last bites of sandwich and side wedge of lettuce, took a swallow of wine and responded: "I am cautious about the outcome at this time, but let me tell you about the day. At the meeting, I first presented a summary of our progress on the project. That included identifying the new specific surface Antigen X on metastatic prostate cancer cells. Next I reviewed our synthesizing Antibody Y to Antigen X, and our progress in using a Nanosphere to enter the small vascular niches in bone where metastatic prostate cancer cells have invaded. I described how the Antibody Y attachment to Antigen X would then allow penetration of an anti-DNA molecule that would kill that cancer cell and prevent its replication."

"I explained that our proposed clinical study would only enroll terminal metastatic prostate cancer patients in which other approaches had failed to stop or heal their bone disease process. Patients would only enter the protocol after they were given full information about it. They would also have the option to withdraw from the study at any time they were dissatisfied with it or felt that we had not treated them fairly."

"Each Committee member then took an opportunity to ask me questions and give opinions. After that, I supplied more in depth experimental details in areas of which they needed clarification. At least two main concerns were raised. One issue was the probable cost of the study, financially and ethically. The feeling by a couple of the Committee was that a more reasonable option might be to encourage placement and retaining of these patients in Palliative and Hospice care programs, instead of our clinical study. This would save Hospital, patient, insurance companies, and research funds many dollars compared to the costs of a person's entering the study."

"I also felt that one or two of the Committee questioned our compassion for patients. That to me seemed to be a pretty subjective implication. Of course, my opinion defends myself, and I realize that I want the study to go forward."

Otto Zellers spoke up: "That sounds like a big day for sure. How many of the 5 on the Committee have to support your proposal for it to pass?"

Moritz replied: "I understand it to be 3 of the 5.

However, Green has not discussed a vote as yet. He has scheduled another meeting to which he has invited an Associate Chairman of the Center's financial group to attend. I am not sure that is good news for me. They might try to delay or halt previously promised funds for me from the Lake View Center's Research Foundation. Although that is not a large amount of money, it could delay the study until I found more extramural funds to cover a financial loss from our Center."

Otto interrupted: "Victor, seems to me that the Committee chair, and maybe the Center, might be trying to de-rail your project. Regarding the cost question, you still have a grant application pending from that pharmaceutical company, which could help pay for some clinical study costs. Have you heard from them yet?"

Moritz shook his head and replied: "Not yet, but expecting word this week. I'm sure that might influence the financial group here at Lake View. However, Otto, listen to this. Rumors are that Green is trying to get our finance Administration to require that a set portion of all awarded science grant money be taken and distributed to promote equality in salary to all members of the Faculty. This is regardless of who wrote the grant, who's productive research led to a successful grant application, the academic rank of the Faculty, or present efforts of Faculty in trying to obtain financial support of their own projects."

"Otto, this seems unfair to me. I can see the Center's Research Foundation receiving a portion of all grants for distribution at times. Yes, there are situations when a Faculty member is having problems with making research progress. Others might need a supplement under certain extenuating circumstances. However, it does not seem moral to confiscate a significant portion of one Faculty's award with the purpose of spreading that awarded money around to try to equalize salaries or research funding levels of all Faculty researchers. Is this a fair goal to promote?"

Obviously having become more agitated as Victor was speaking about this grant money distribution plan, Otto shouted: "Victor, we can see what they are up to with this plan. This is a brazen attempt to introduce a wedge into this Center's core philosophy. Which is, or was, one's right to reap the yields of their own efforts. Wage controls, attempting to take a person's work and make it the property of society, in this case the whole science Faculty, is wrong. It suggests that your reason for existence is not to work for your own sake. No, on the contrary, you should live to do service for all the other members of the science Faculty attempting research at this Center."

"Also, such an approach would likely lead towards an attitude of mediocracy. At least a portion of the Faculty would be inclined to think, why work so hard to put themselves out in front of others in an area of expertise? Many, in this situation developing here, would not exert a harder effort to find a cure, or a cause of cancer, if all those working here were receiving the same financial awards."

"The result? The scientific level of research at this Institution would then fall because of removing the incentive of recognition for one's own accomplishments. I know, we are only talking, in part, about money here. However, starting this mindset would lead to lower motivation and less interest in the challenge of science among many of our Faculty. This Center would overall slide toward mediocracy instead of standing among the leaders in many ongoing cancer research efforts like yours. I know that some of the Faculty would still work their hardest to excel, regardless of the grant money distribution and politics. But overall, the Center would change, believe me."

Victor Moritz thoughtfully considered what Otto Zellers had just spoke about. He then said slowly:

"Yes, I agree with your concerns. I am wondering if it really can be happening and wish I could do something to stop it. However, right now I will continue to work my hardest to get extramural grant money for our research. If the Nanosphere Complex approach is helpful for patients with metastatic prostate cancer to bone, I will apply for a Patent. That would help add research money for others at Lake View. For now, my focus is to stick to the goal of seeing my clinical study begin and succeed."

Moritz then said, taking a big sigh: "Otto, let's talk about something else for a while."

***

Zellers responded, also seeming happy to change the subject: "Well you want to change the subject, let me lay something on you that I think about often."

"Victor, to tell you the truth, this growing old isn't always a breeze. I definitely am slowing down physically, compared to what I used to be. At the gym, or even the grocery store, I see others moving quickly, not limping, hurrying to the next piece of equipment or food shelf. Sometimes, privately, I hold resentment towards them and their active life styles and ease of movements. I might even feel angry inside myself towards a person I don't even know, because they went over and picked up the set of dumbbells I was just going to use in my next exercise. Sometimes I even feel resentment, or frustration, seeing someone working fast and hard on the treadmill, while I can barely walk on it at the lowest rate setting on the machine."

"I approach each closed door in public with caution for fear that someone will come bursting through as they are hurrying to get to their next event, meeting, or whatever. After I dodge a rapidly thrown open door, it even makes me angrier if the person is talking on their cell phone, and being unaware of any concern for others, looking down while sending or receiving a Text or e-mail".

"Then at other times, I feel the need to almost apologize to those I am impatient with or irritated by. They are just living their life as they are capable of. They have no clue that I am irritated about anything. Rather, I should be happy for them being young and in good health. In order to compensate for my negative feelings, I sometimes slow down my walking, just so it makes it easier for a rushing person to pass by me. Or I might try to disguise my limping, or even stop walking, just to avoid having someone hold the door open for me before they go in."

"Other things get to me. How about when I become irritated with myself when I am changing out of a pair of shoes into a pair of slippers and I step on the shoe strings so the shoes fall out of my hand when trying to put them in the closet. I notice that I drop things a lot more than I used to- utensils, food, tools, dental floss, clothing and so on. Then, I have to slowly bend over to pick the stuff up."

Victor was listening attentively. He spoke with compassion in his voice: "I can imagine that such feelings and frustrations occur for you. But this likely happens to most of us as we age, to one degree or another. I remember my Dad and Mom, when they were getting older, expressing similar feelings."

Zellers went on: "Yes, and that isn't all. I am losing many of my long time acquaintances and friends as they are passing with regularity now it seems. All my teachers and mentors are gone. News of the passing of peers, previous competitors, work associates, and others is always coming up in Alumni publications, newspapers, and conversations with friends. Other apparent losses are suggested when letters I send are returned undelivered"

"Victor, I can't say exactly that I dwell on it constantly, but at least once a day I think about dying. How will it happen? Will it be heart, stroke, accident, suddenly or slowly, and where at? Am I sure that all my wishes are clarified and recorded, so my daughter, remaining few relatives, or others responsible, will be able to handle my death without anxiety, frustration and anger because my requests were left in a mess?"

"These thoughts can come up at any time. They can occur working at an odd job, weeding in the garden, being in the gym, or loafing around the house. Sometimes, if I am fortunate enough to get good results on the studies my Doctor has ordered, I am afraid to feel too good about it. At other times if I finish a job that took a hard amount of effort and I am feeling good about it, I pause and tell myself not to get overconfident or feel too satisfied. I suddenly remember that my body and physiology might easily change all that satisfaction. Just the next minute, there could be a trip to the Emergency Room, a hospital bed for days, or the morgue. You don't always know when you are going to get kicked below the belt."

"What will happen to my things like memos of family and profession? Should I even care, such things will not have the same sentiment and meaning to anyone else but me. Although I can understand that, it is still bothersome. I will just hope that my daughter, Amy, will select a few pictures, mementos, books or antiques to pass on to the next generation. It might help them remember a bit of my life and times."

"Oh Victor, things have changed so much in my lifetime. Not just the advancements in the mechanics of our day, such as communication networking, fast lifestyle pace, and scientific developments. Also, there has been a decline, as I see it, in manners and respect for one another, for example. It seems like a lot of people are in a real big hurry."

"Victor, am I suffering from depression that occurs frequently in elderly people like me?"

Victor took his and Otto's plates to the kitchen sink, then returned to Otto at the table, saying: "Well, as you point out, Otto, the elderly certainly can become depressed, even so severely that some commit suicide. Yes, you are slowing down and have more aches and pains than you did when you were younger. However, I don't think you are near being seriously depressed. I have never heard you say that your sleeping and daily routine habits have changed. You don't seem to be breaking plans with your friends and withdrawing socially. Your weight is stable. The hip pain is real, and not imaginary. Talking as we are now, you seem rational and focused, not absent minded, irritable, or easily distracted from an issue before us, as we are speaking."

"I do sense that you have the occasional feeling of being worthless, and have some self-pity and guilty feelings, but these seem like relatively brief events. With all your interests and activities you are engaged in, I don't think you are experiencing anything close to significant depression. Keep up the good work, friend."

Otto seemed somewhat reassured after hearing what Victor had to say about his concern of depression. After another hour of talking,   Victor Moritz said good night to Otto and left for his home in the country, about 30 minutes from Lake View Medical Center.

5

It was dark when Victor left Otto's home. He felt good that they had a frank talk, and he had appreciated his friend's opinions and perception of what might be going on with the Committee review of his study protocol. Also, maybe it was true that there was a hidden agenda within some Faculty members at the Center, which might ultimately change its character and productivity.

Hearing Otto talk about aging brought back the memory of his own father, who had steadily failed with increasing lung fibrosis and a low heart rate, despite being treated with a pacemaker. Eventually these two issues negatively affected multiple organ systems causing his father's death. Victor thought he had been reasonable in response to Otto's concern about possibly getting serious depression with his aging. However, Victor made a mental note to himself to keep this in mind when he visited his friend from time to time.

The drive home usually took about 30 minutes, a rather winding road through farming country, then arriving at his modern cabin on 40 acres. There were two 5-6 acre cleared pastures, an acre of orchard, and about 27 acres of hilly woodlands. Shortly into his drive tonight, Moritz's thoughts pleasantly drifted to a subject he spent time thinking about each day, his relationship with Ruth.

***

A year ago at a National Cancer Society meeting in Denver, Victor and Ruth met while attending a symposium. On the second day of the meeting, Victor had presented some of his research at one of the lecture sessions. Ruth had approached him afterwards to ask for some clarification of one of his points in the lecture. At the time, Victor had been a widower for 4 years.

Victor had rarely thought about any type of serious relationship with another women since Rachel's accidental death. This meeting of Victor and Ruth, she now 32 years old, had come roughly 3 years after Ruth had divorced. Her husband had worked for the Environmental Protection Agency, and was in charge of implementing certain regulations concerning water treatment for a portion of Arizona, including Phoenix. Ruth had wanted children but he did not. There were other issues as well. He had started drinking frequently with friends after work and coming home obviously having had too many alcoholic drinks. In this shape, he was irritable towards Ruth and they frequently then had serious arguments, even to the point where he had started slapping her around on some of these occasions. He then began secretly seeing another woman from his office group. He and Ruth tried couples therapy, but that did not improve their situation. After months of this, Ruth, having had enough pain, returned the wedding ring, filed for and was granted a divorce.

On the third day of the Denver meeting, Victor and Ruth, not yet knowing the other's past, saw one another at the evening social hour. They approached each other, exchanged greetings and started a conversation. That had ended in their going out to dinner that evening. They found a quiet restaurant a block from the busy Convention Center Hotel. Conversation during dinner was relaxed and they began to learn each other's background, interests, likes and dislikes fairly well over the casual meal. One of their common interests, they found, was hiking as often as possible. As it happened, they had both brought their hiking shoes and light backpacks in case of an opportunity for some hiking during the week of the conference. The conversation surprisingly led to their planning on a 1-2 day mini trip for a hiking experience in the Rocky Mountains. After dinner, and saying goodnight to Ruth, Victor arranged for a rental vehicle, hiking poles for two, water containers and snacking supplies for a day hike.

The vendors were fortunately located adjacent to the hotel in which the meeting was occurring.

The next morning, Victor and Ruth met in the hotel lobby for coffee and an early breakfast. A little after 6:30 AM, they were heading for Grays Peak, a popular and not too difficult mountain to hike, yet with a 14,278 foot high summit. Grays was only about a one hour drive West of Denver on Interstate 70. The exit for access to Grays Peak was at Bakerville. Next was a 3-1/2 mile rough dirt and stone road to the parking lot and the trailhead. Victor was glad he had rented a 4 wheel drive Jeep for the trip because it had been a rough stretch of road up to the parking lot.

From the parking lot, about 4 miles from the mountain's summit, the trail's switchbacks, although gaining elevation gradually, had been pretty easy for about 3 miles. After that, the trail soon began to get tougher. Views of the distant summit were deceiving with the suggestion of being close, but there were still many switchbacks, and the grade was steeper as Ruth and Victor continued. They had been lucky that where there was snow, a partially packed trail by others had helped. It was warm enough that there was no ice pack to slip on. They had seen 3 mountain goats barely 10 yards away as they came around one switchback corner. Other people were also hiking on parts of the trail, and Victor wondered if some of those were also possibly from the conference in Denver. The final part of the hike was all rock scrambling to the summit, which had to be done with care, and pausing a couple of times for a short rest and water break.

The views on the trail were awesome in themselves. However, views in all directions from the summit were even more stunning. Long distances of mountain range and peaks seemed endless. Victor and Ruth looked at each other, slowly shaking their heads, with obvious amazement at the sights. They spent over a half hour just viewing the beauty from all edges of the summit and sitting down to rest on readily available rock edges. After a light snack and water, they started the descent. The hike down was somewhat easier, but one still had to take care. They arrived back at the parking lot at 3:00 PM, roughly six hours after starting at the trailhead.

After the exhilarating, challenging, and tiring summit of Grays Peak, the two rested and used the facilities at the parking lot. During the descent, they had talked about what the plan might be for the evening. Victor said that one of the persons he had met at the conference told him the small community of Dillon, about 30 miles west of Grays' access road, had a large water reservoir with very nice views of the shoreline and mountains. After a short discussion of that, and comparing it to driving back to a crowded convention and late afternoon traffic in Denver, they decided to go to Dillon.

There was still daylight in the waning afternoon to enjoy mountain views while on the highway, and the scenic Eisenhower-Johnson Memorial Tunnel. They arrived in Dillon at a motel located on the water reservoir in the early evening, as the sun was sliding down behind the mountain peaks. Ruth and Victor obtained separate rooms in the motel and each had good mountain views from the outside walkway to their rooms.

***

During dinner at a nearby Bistro, they had a personal, open, and sensitive discussion of their lives, including backgrounds and loves lost. They also shared their professional settings and aspirations.

Ruth was the oldest of the three children in her family. Both parents had worked at steady blue collar jobs, but raising 3 children required a tight budget and sparse spending on some extras that more affluent families were able to enjoy.

Ruth had a part time job while in High School, working in the housekeeping services of the local Hospital. She saved much of that income. That savings and awards from the Nursing School of the nearby College, given for her academic excellence, aided her in being accepted to and attending the Nursing School.

Ruth's motivation for a nursing career came in part from watching firsthand the cares and performance of the nursing staff when working part time at the Hospital while in High School. In addition, her younger brother suffered acute leukemia when he was 12 years old. Thus, she had seen suffering first hand. Thankfully, her brother had been in remission already 5 years when she was graduating with her Bachelor's and Registered Nurse degrees. Now, Ruth had a Master's Degree and specialized in Pediatric cancer care Nursing.

Ruth's work was primarily in Hospital clinical care. In addition, however, she makes an effort to attend a yearly State or National Cancer Society meeting. She does this to learn more about basic cancer biology and new developments in therapeutic medications and cares. She feels that additional background knowledge in these basic areas will help her understand her patient's condition with a wider perspective while dealing with the clinical nursing issues. Her supervisor and Director of Nursing at the Hospital she now works at in Phoenix agrees. In fact, the Nursing Department financially supports her trips in this endeavor to compliment clinical bedside nursing skills and information. As part of the arrangement with the Hospital, she is then required to submit a report to the Hospital Nursing administration and summarize the new concepts she learned at these conferences for other members of the Hospital's cancer care Nurses. Victor complimented Ruth on this effort and thought that it was something he might suggest to the Nursing management at Lake View

About halfway to his home, Victor's thoughts were interrupted briefly by a fox successfully dashing across the road in front of his vehicle. After this alert, Victor continued remembering more of his first warm encounter with Ruth.

Walking back to the motel, Victor and Ruth had spontaneously reached for each other's hand, and walked holding hands back to the edge of the shoreline. They stopped for a moment enjoying the clear crisp evening air. Though not spoken, each quietly felt a respectful and close sentiment developing between them. After walking up the steps to the rooms, Victor paused at Ruth's door, then said goodnight. Hesitating before turning to his room next door, he asked if she wanted to eat breakfast together. Ruth answered that she would like that very much, and then they said goodnight.

At breakfast they both admitted to having a few tender and stiff leg muscles, though fortunately no foot blisters. Afterwards, they took a walk to an outside bench and sat. The view of the surrounding mountain scenery was again impressive and they both agreed that leaving the conference for a break had turned out to be a great experience.

***

Arriving back at the conference hotel before noon, Victor let Ruth out to go to her room, while he returned the Jeep and other items to the vendor. Returning to his room, he showered, dressed for the evening, took his notebook and pen and went to a couple of afternoon symposia sessions on topics relevant to his own research interests. Between sessions, he had contacted Ruth and they agreed to have dinner together again that evening.

When the second symposium ended at 7:00 PM, Victor and Ruth met and had dinner together in the hotel's restaurant. After their meal, they took a walk, and then went to Ruth's room and made love. Each had slowly explored the other's body, found ecstatic and compete satisfaction in their climaxes and sincere close feelings for each other, which they expressed.

In the morning after packing, they met at breakfast before setting off on their separate transportation schedules back to their homes and work. Victor told Ruth that what happened between them the last two days had touched him more than superficially. He wanted to see her again. He asked if she possibly would think it over. Victor said he realized the distance between their locations, her work, his work, call schedules and research all would make it difficult, but maybe they could manage some sort of communication and test their feelings further. Ruth expressed that she had a similar interest in seeing and being with him again, and they should try it.

During this past year after they first met, Victor had flown to see Ruth in Tempe on 3 week-ends, one each in October, February and June. In between, they usually talked by phone every week or so, varying somewhat on each ones longing for contact with the other.

On the first visit in October, most of the time was spent in Ruth's apartment in Tempe. They just walked through the neighborhood and parks nearby. They had also tried golfing once, but as they expected, neither was particularly good at it, not being that interested in it to begin with. During the February visit, they went to a desert flower and cactus garden display one morning. After that, they hiked up Camelback Mountain. At the top of this 2700 foot high landmark, there was a quiet and peaceful experience as they looked out over the area surrounding Phoenix. At each of these visits, they had time to eat out or cook in, depending on their mood. They also saw and toured the Hospital where Ruth worked. Quiet evenings of talking, listening to music and making love continued to be a pleasant experience for both.

In June, Victor and Ruth drove to the south rim of the Grand Canyon, hiked down Bright Angel Trail, and stayed overnight at Phantom Ranch. They did a couple of short hikes during the next day, and hiked back out Bright Angel after the second night.

**

Victor's thoughts on this, now serious relationship, were set aside as he turned into the lane leading up to his cabin. He was glad to be home after quite a long day. The eyes of his 4 beef cattle shown as the car's headlights caught them in the pasture by the fence. As he neared the yard, he heard the barking of his black Labrador, Shadow, anxiously awaiting his master's return from the day's long absence.

Victor was glad that Ruth was visiting him here at the cabin this weekend. This was the first time she had been able to visit him since beginning their relationship. The timing of the Committee Meeting had come up after their arrangements for this weekend had been made. Victor and Ruth had decided this would not matter, as it was due time for them to see each other again. Visiting Victor at his place was something both were really looking forward to.

6

Next morning was the clinic visit for Jim Davis to see Dr. Moritz. Jim wanted to be one of the first patients receiving the Nanosphere Complex, pending the outcome of the Patient Care and Research Ethics Committee decision.

Of course, this was not Jim Davis's first time in the clinic. He had been there initially 4 years ago for diagnosis and starting treatments of his primary prostate cancer at age of 50. The cancer appeared to respond after each of 3 separate chemotherapy and radiation trials, but returned with vengeance. Extensive metastases had now been found in the bones of his legs and spine.

Jim was a successful small businessman. When 20 years old, he satisfied his passion of baking sweets for himself by starting a small bakery in the town near the Lake View Center. Through the hard work of himself, his wife, Rita, their two children, and faithful employees from the community, the business grew in sales and popularity.

Jim had been a stout and robust man until 4 years ago. Now with the ravages of his invasive cancer metastases, he was frail, stooped, weak, and weighed only 135 pounds on his 5 foot, 11 inch frame. He was using a cane to help manage his unsteady balance and walking, due to the pain and weakness in his legs from the cancer now in those bones. Rita was helping steady Jim and get him comfortable as they found chairs in the clinic waiting room.

Rita was an attractive 5 feet 5 inch woman. She had long brown hair to match her brown eyes. Her walk was natural and unforced, yet seductive. It appeared as if her body was gliding gracefully towards whatever was ahead of her. Legs, hips, breasts, arms, head and eyes all flowing together. Rita was 5 years younger than Jim. Both were from local families, and stayed close to their hometown after High School. Jim, already in his established business 6 years, proposed to Rita when she turned 21. They had formed a close friendship and respect for each other during the previous 3 years that Rita had worked in the bakery after her high school graduation. She had then assumed most of the daily responsibilities of the bakery functioning within a couple years after marrying Jim. This allowed Jim to continue to work on new baking ideas, have hands on management of the finances, taking care of supplies and training employees, so things were good.

Jim and Rita's children had moved forward in their chosen professions after college, located to other states, married and had families. Jim's elderly parents had passed during the time Jim was in his first year of cancer treatments.

Consequently, Rita had become responsible for managing all of the bakery business, caring and support for Jim, and seeing that their home was clean and comfortable. Jim's health now had continued to deteriorate, despite all cares he was receiving. Therefore, they had sold the bakery a few months ago to a younger couple from the area.

***

The waiting rooms in the Cancer Clinic were not cheerful scenes. The check-in desks usually had 2 or 3 patients in line for each of the receptionists. The first waiting room was where patients sat and waited to be called to the clinic laboratory to have blood drawn for studies that would help with their evaluation. After returning from the laboratory, patients remained in this waiting room until called for their clinic appointment with their Oncologist. Jim and Rita were now waiting for Jim's turn in the laboratory today.

Another waiting room, separated from the laboratory and first clinic waiting room, received patients that were undergoing treatments that day. Treatments could be 4-6 hours of intravenous chemotherapy, immunotherapy, or other medications, and procedures such as a spinal tap or bone marrow aspiration. These patients were cared for in private rooms separated from one another, and were large enough to facilitate the patient's bed, the equipment needed for therapy, the treating nursing and medical staff, and the patient's support person or persons.

It was usually easy to tell the clinic's patients from their support persons. Patients wearing a hat covering their total hair loss from chemotherapy was common. Some were wearing a mask to avoid getting a respiratory infection. This was also common and important because the blood cells that fight infection are frequently decreased by either the patient's disease or their chemotherapy or radiation treatments.

Patients in wheel chairs were frequent. Jim and Rita watched a man pushing a wheelchair with his frail wife holding on. They both had gray hair, both wore breast cancer pink tee shirts. This said clearly that the wife had breast cancer. The husband's tee shirt made a statement that he was trying to support her fight against this disease. He found a place for the wheelchair beside his chair and a stand with magazines. After she was settled, he brought them both a cup of coffee that was available in the waiting room. Rita had been similarly attentive to Jim, but had him settled in a chair fairly close to the doors to the blood work laboratory. She had also brought them both coffee and a sugar cookie from the room's free snack counter.

About 15 minutes after arriving, it was Jim's turn to have blood drawn. The blood sampling and analyses would help assist Dr. Moritz to follow Jim's progress. When his name was called, Rita helped Jim up, handed him his cane and assisted him in walking to the door of the laboratory. Then the laboratory technician guided Jim to a reclining chair for the blood drawing, while Rita returned to the waiting room. After the procedure, the technician assisted Jim back to his chair beside Rita in the waiting room. It would be about an hour now for the blood analyses to be completed. Then he would be called into Dr. Moritz's examining room.

Jim now relaxed a little and took a look around the room. It was nearly full and he started a mental note of this assembly at a Cancer Clinic. A younger man, thin, limping and wearing a baseball cap, was just sitting down. In a couple of minutes, he was joined by a woman who appeared to be his wife. He immediately held out his hand and she took it as she sat down beside him. They then drew closer on the double chair and started talking quietly together. At least a half dozen others in the clinic were texting, engaged in e-mail exchanges or using information webs on their cell phones. One was working on their laptop computer and two were reading paperback books.

Of interest to Jim was a man on his cell phone constantly chatting about yesterday's sporting news. He carried on his phone chatting, instead of talking with the woman patient he came into the clinic with, apparently not even thinking about helping her off with her coat. Jim thought that was very selfish and inconsiderate of that man. The newspaper and magazine rack contents in the room were not very popular today. The TV was on a news channel, low volume, in one corner of the room with three persons watching it.

Jim noted that, as usual, some patients were sharing their cancer experiences in conversation with others. Diagnosis, treatments, progress or prognosis and their Doctor's names were being discussed. Jim had never felt comfortable entering such conversations himself, and he turned to Rita and gave her a wink and nudge. She knew he was reminding her they had discussed his reluctance to do this.

One group today could not be missed. About

seven or eight people occupied a large number of chairs along one wall of the room. They had spread out and there was, what seemed like to Jim, 2 or 3 separate conversations going on at once within this group. Talking loudly, waving their arms, at least 2 or 3 speaking at the same time, often even essentially shouting to be heard at the other end of the group. It was unclear to Jim which of the group, if any, was the patient. Several of the other waiting room persons, including Jim and Rita, found this behavior disturbing, and even inappropriate. To top it all off, two of the group had their hands full of and each were consuming 4-6 cookies from the patient treats counter by the coffee pot. They had been back to refill their hands more than once. All snacks were now gone until more would arrive in the late afternoon.

Jim's thoughts were initially critical of this apparent rudeness of noise and consumption of nearly all of the whole waiting room's snacks. Yet he reconsidered and thought maybe the group was actually just exhibiting joy after hearing that a friend or family member with them had been cured of a cancerous process. That would be good news to celebrate. On the other hand, possibly they were manifesting anxiety behavior from worrying about possible bad news coming to one of their family members at this clinic visit.

In contrast to this group, Jim and Rita both were struck by an awesome display of support and sympathy they had never seen before. A mother, bald from chemotherapy, was accompanied by a younger woman, who looked like she was her daughter. She had a full head of long hair. After some apparently serious conversation between them, they hugged, side by side. The daughter with the long hair took her hand and placed her hair up and over the bald head of her mother and held it there for a solemn, comforting and sincere moment. Shortly after, both shed tears for a few minutes. They then separated from their hug, the younger woman put her hair back in place, and they resumed their conversation. This had also brought tears to Jim and Rita's eyes.

***

About 45 minutes after his blood work was drawn, a clinic Nurse called Jim's name. Rita and Jim made their way to her at the entrance to the clinic offices and exam rooms. The Nurse said, smiling at Jim, as was usually the case: "How are you?"

Jim, obviously struggling to even walk, responded: "OK I guess." Jim had always thought it would be better if the Nurses would say: 'Good to see you, Jim' or 'Happy you are able to make it in today.' Somehow, Jim thought that something could be said that was more welcoming, personal, and slightly uplifting, rather than a joyful 'How are you' in this clinic where serious disease was sitting everywhere.

After Jim was weighed, the nurse directed him and Rita to the room to see Dr. Moritz. The blood pressure, pulse and temperature measurements were first. Next was a confirmation of Jim's present medications, and a review of how he had been doing since last in the clinic 2 weeks ago. The Nurse then completed her questioning, asked if Jim or Rita needed anything at this time, told them Dr. Moritz would be in shortly, and then left the room.

Dr. Victor Moritz arrived less than 5 minutes later. He rinsed his hands with antibacterial solution, dried them, and then greeted and shook hands with Jim and Rita. He had a brief feeling that Rita held on to his hand a little longer than usual, but he didn't think much more of it at the time. He asked them to try to relax and be as calm as possible, knowing that they were anxious to hear about the results of the Committee meeting.

Over the next several minutes, Moritz explained what had happened at the Committee meeting yesterday. He shared with them his overall assessment. He tried to point out that this first meeting, had in reality, only been the start in the process of obtaining approval for beginning his clinical study. He had expected a quicker approval, but had to abide by the Center's regulations and procedure.

However, Jim and Rita took the news of more meetings as an obvious setback for them. Jim was anxious to get on with the experimental trial. He cursed at the bureaucracy of the Center holding out like this for reasons that he thought were only tactics to delay and frustrate him, Dr. Moritz, and other potential candidates for the study.

After a few minutes of sharing their disappointment about the Committee meeting, Dr. Moritz said a few words about the next scheduled meeting. The fact that Green was bringing in someone from the Center's finance department to participate in the approval process made the desperate Davis couple even angrier at their situation. Again, Moritz empathized with them, but kept trying to convince them to be as understanding with the situation as possible. He promised that he would do everything in his power to make a good case for his study.

Moritz then shifted their discussion to the other important purpose of this office visit, Jim's present health status and progress over the last 2 weeks.

Moritz, reading today's lab results, said: "Jim, many of today's lab results are within normal range. However, a new finding is that your blood Cortisol level was very low today compared to levels on past tests. Also, your blood sugar, that is, glucose, value was lower than usual. The nurse had also said you seemed weaker than at last visit. Finally, your blood pressure today was markedly lower than it usually is. Let me first do my physical examination, and then we will talk more about what these observations might mean."

Jim, shaking his head, said: "Sounds like more bad news, Doc."

Moritz examined Jim thoroughly. Possibly, he found some increase in Jim's overall weakness due to his cachectic, or wasted, condition accompanying his spreading cancer bone metastases. The neurologic part of the exam was normal, except for the weakness, nothing specific pointed to a change in brain function.

After the physical examination, Dr. Moritz picked up a tablet and pen to draw with, then sat down with Jim and Rita and began:

"Jim, there is something wrong with your level of a major hormone which is made in your adrenal glands. This hormone is called Cortisol, also called a glucocorticoid. We assessed this hormone by measuring your blood Cortisol level. Your level is very low today. As I am showing you in my sketch here, the adrenal glands are important organs that are located on the upper pole of each kidney. The adrenals are influenced by another gland, the pituitary gland, which is located within your skull. There are several possible reasons for low Cortisol levels."

"One possibility is that a hemorrhage or infection has occurred in your adrenal glands and so they cannot make regular amounts of Cortisol. A second possibility is that the pituitary gland, which is located just below your brain, is injured and not sending a message to the adrenal glands to make more Cortisol. A third possibility, unfortunately, is that your prostate cancer has metastasized to yet another organ, either the adrenals or the pituitary gland."

Moritz looked at Jim and his wife: "Are you two following me so far?"

Both Jim and Rita nodded yes, and Jim said: "I think so. The diagram you drew while talking to us helped a lot. Which one of the options is the problem?"

Dr. Moritz went on: "Jim, we need to find this out as quickly as possible. Lack of Cortisol has many bad effects. It can lead to very low blood pressure and shock if you have a sudden new stress occurrence. This is called an 'adrenal crisis'. In addition, it can contribute to very low blood sugar levels, further weakness, and more."

After a short pause, Dr. Moritz continued: "Jim, I want to admit you to the Hospital right now. We would obtain radiographic scans of various types to locate possible metastases to the adrenals or pituitary. We would do further blood work to help determine whether it is primarily a problem in the adrenal glands, or a problem from the lack of pituitary function. We will start you on Cortisol and other adrenal hormone replacement medications as soon as drawing the blood for tests is completed. We will work on some other things, such as trying ways to improve your nutrition, for example. I expect you would be in the Hospital for 4-5 days, possibly being discharged on Monday."

"I know this is sudden and once again bad news for the two of you. I am very sorry to give you this news that adds onto your already serious medical situation. Take a few minutes to talk about this together. I will visit another patient, and then be back to see you and answer more questions if you have them."

***

After Moritz left, Rita reached for Jim's hand and held it firmly, tears starting to form in her eyes as she looked at him. She remembered that she had thought Jim was looking and acting weaker the last few days, and appearing a shade paler than he usually looked. She was worried about him.

Rita then spoke up: "Jim, the final decision is yours on whether or not you go into the Hospital again, even though it sounds like only a 4-5 day stay. Either way, it seems like another serious problem has come up. Maybe it is not cancer spreading further, maybe it is a less serious problem that can be treated with adding the adrenal medications. I am wishing that is the case."

Jim squeezed her hand gently, and then reached over and ran his hand and fingers over her head and through her hair, following it down to her shoulders and back.

He said: "Rita, I do love you so much. I am sorry my illness is taking so much out of us both. You have been so caring and considerate of my frailties caused by this cancer and the negative side effects of therapies. I know it has strained our marriage and personal relationship a great deal."

He continued, now dropping her hair and slamming his fist down on the arm of his chair: "I am sometimes ready to give up, forget Dr. Moritz's study and his new Nanosphere approach, stop eating, increase the pain medications beyond drowsy, and just pass away."

Rita said nothing, but reached for and found his hand again. She now realized that Jim's eyes were red, watery, and that he was also crying.

Jim then went on speaking: "But, you know, maybe some good could come by hanging in there and entering Dr. Moritz's study. If he gets approval I might contribute, even some small amount, to knowledge about bone metastases. So, Rita my companion and love, I think I should be admitted to the Hospital today and get the scans and tests. If possible, I hope to live long enough to enter his clinical study. For some reason, I believe Dr. Moritz will win over the Committee and gain their permission to start enrolling patients. I hope you will continue to support me in this decision."

Rita said without hesitation: "Of course, and I want those Nanospheres to work their way to your diseased bones and destroy those cancer cells. I hope others in the study also benefit, and that this is a significant step in the fight against cancer metastases to bone. Yes, the situation is hard on me too, as you said just now, but I am your wife and partner for better or worse."

Although weak, Jim leaned as far as he could towards Rita so they could have at least a partial embrace, despite the awkwardness of the chair spacing and office furnishings. It then was quiet between them for a few minutes, until Dr. Moritz returned to the room.

Moritz said: "Tell me any concerns, opinions, or questions that you have and I will try to answer you as best as I can."

Jim, looking at Rita while he spoke: "Dr. Moritz, we are together in thinking I ought to get admitted into the Hospital as soon as possible. We need to find out what is going on so I can still hopefully get to enter your proposed clinical study."

Dr. Moritz said he would support and care for them as best as he was able. Then he went to the computer and wrote orders for Jim's Hospital admission and studies that needed to be carried out.

When finished with that, Moritz said: "I will keep you both informed of the results of the tests as soon as they are available. I may discuss some results with a couple other doctors in my Department if needed. The Nurse will arrange for a transport person and wheelchair for you that will make it easier to get to the Hospital rooms. Best of luck to you both."

Jim and Rita thanked Dr. Moritz again for his help as he was leaving the room to return to other clinic patients.

7

After making the arrangements for Jim's admission to the Hospital, Dr. Moritz continued seeing and caring for his clinic patients until noon. He then went to the weekly Oncology Grand Rounds. Here, the Oncology Department's Faculty, Residents, Fellows and Students attend a lecture given by an invited guest speaker. These Grand Rounds' speakers were regularly well established in their specialty. They presented state of the art information through a 45-60 minute lecture, followed by a few minutes of answering questions from the audience. Moritz had some trouble focusing on the presented material this day, as his mind drifted back to events of the last 36 hours.

However, Moritz had respect for the visitor's expertise and he became attentive. The speaker was reporting progress to identify a specific Antigen marker present on ovarian cancer cells. This could possibly be studied further and eventually lead to a specific and reliable diagnosis in the early stages of ovarian cancer. The subject was an important one since ovarian cancer is often far advanced and has already metastasized when the diagnosis is made. That results in a very high death rate in ovarian cancer patients. There was enthusiastic interest in his findings, and several questions followed the lecture.

$$***$$

Dr. Moritz returned to his clinic patients after the seminar, and finished with clinic at a little after 5:00 PM. He signed out with the clinic staff and went over to the Oncology ward to check on Jim Davis.

Moritz reviewed the results of the afternoon's studies that were now available. He discussed Jim's cares thus far since admission to the ward with the Nurse in charge and the Oncology Resident responsible for patient care today. He then went in to see Jim. Jim had experienced an exhaustive day since leaving the clinic in the morning. He had brain and adrenal studies in the Radiology Department and an exam in the Neurology Department. Intravenous medications were given and blood drawing as necessary was done. He had been placed on various vital sign monitors. Jim had been moved from bed to wheel chair for transport to the various sites in the Hospital for these studies.

Dr. Moritz said: "Jim, I know it has been a hard day for you. Are you handling it as best as you can?"

Jim in a weak voice, adjusting his position in bed,

responded. "It's okay Dr. Moritz. Yes, it has been hard, but I am committed with you to find out what this recent problem is."

Moritz sat down at Jim's bedside, then said: "Jim, we do have a few answers. First, the brain studies are normal. No evidence of cancer metastases affecting your pituitary or other parts of your brain. Also, the Neurologist found no alarming findings on his physical examination at this time, other than those clearly the result of your debilitated status from your cancer and treatments you already have undergone."

"Second, the scan of your adrenal glands shows that there is hemorrhage present. This is not due to cancer metastases. It is due to something else. Often we do not know what causes adrenal hemorrhage. We will do some more laboratory tests to help us find the cause in your case. This will include blood coagulation factors, and maybe some other studies as well."

"The hemorrhage into the adrenal glands has deceased their ability to produce essential hormones that have very significant roles in your blood pressure, stress response, salt balance, blood sugar, and your energy level. We can treat these symptoms with medications, some of which I have already ordered for you. You should be feeling better in a few days, but we will need to use these new medications until the bleeding into your adrenal glands stops and for an extended period afterwards. We will retest your adrenal laboratory values from time to time to follow how much adrenal function returns as the hemorrhage site resolves and repairs. If good repair occurs, we can reduce some of medication doses. Overall, I am very happy this is not another metastasis, and we hope to get you stable and out of the Hospital by the first of the week."

Jim, with somewhat more spirit in his voice, said: "Doc, thanks again for all your help. I feel a little better hearing the news you just told me. Use your own judgement on when you think I should be discharged."

"Now, I have a couple other things I need to say to you this evening.   First, if you think it might help, I would be glad to go to one of the Committee meetings, if I am able, and say something supportive about your Nanosphere study. At least give it a thought. Second, if you have time, would you stop by and talk to Rita about these recent results. You could explain them to her and discuss your plans. She left the hospital before these studies today, and I think she is really worried."

"Rita seemed pretty exhausted and in a down mood with my latest deterioration. She said she was not planning on coming back to the hospital until tomorrow morning. Our children, in other States, are consumed with their own families and work responsibilities, so they are not helping support their Mother very much."

Moritz said to Jim: "I will be getting a sandwich at the Hospital cafeteria and then work in the office until about 7:00 PM. Then I can certainly stop by your place and talk with Rita, if that is acceptable with both of you. Have the Nurse call me on my cell phone if it is not convenient at that time. In any event, I will be checking on you tomorrow morning. Jim, try to get a good night's rest."

Jim said he was confident that it would be fine to visit Rita this evening, but he would call her to be sure. They shook hands, Dr. Moritz left the room and headed for the elevator and the cafeteria.

***

It was after 7:30 PM when Dr. Moritz rang Jim and Rita Davis' doorbell. Rita was dressed in casual fitted sweats, having changed from her clothes worn to the Hospital this morning. She was holding a nearly empty glass of red wine, and smiled rather weakly. She told Moritz that Jim had called about his suggesting that Dr. Moritz drop by to give her an update on his condition and plans for further studies.

She said: "Dr. Moritz, please come in. Thank you for coming."

Moritz said, as he entered: "Hi Rita, I am glad to be able to come and talk with you."

Rita led them into the living room, saying: "Have a seat wherever you would like. I will bring in a plate of crackers and cheese if you feel like a snack. I am going to pour myself another glass of wine. Would you like a glass also? Or some coffee or hot tea?"

Moritz, for a moment, remembered how Rita had held on to his hand a little longer than he expected during their handshake this morning in clinic. Then he let the thought pass.

He said: "A cup of hot tea would be great if it isn't too much of a bother."

"No problem at all. I'll just use the microwave for the hot water, and will bring you a choice of black or green tea bags." Rita speaking as she walked to the kitchen.

Moritz took a corner of the angled sofa near the coffee table, which had a clear view of the house's open kitchen. He watched Rita in the kitchen, her movements, natural and confident, underscored her sensuality. He thought of how very attractive she was. Before Rita could notice him staring, Victor Moritz sat back in the sofa, looked away from the kitchen, and focused his thoughts on the purpose of his visit to this home.

Within a few minutes, Rita returned with a tray of snacks, hot water and tea bags for Moritz, and her glass of wine. She then sat down facing Moritz in another nearby chair. She crossed her legs and arranged her exercise outfit, which clearly emphasized her figure.

Rita said: "Dr. Moritz, what are Jim's studies showing? Is there, and will I be able to take, more bad news?"

Moritz responded: "Rita, the news is mixed. The brain scan was normal, no cancer there. That is very good news. The other scan of significance showed adrenal gland hemorrhages. Again, that is also good news, since there was no evidence of prostate cancer metastases involved in the adrenal glands. We can treat the adrenal hemorrhage, but it requires some time and additional medications."

Moritz went on to explain Jim's condition in more detail. He went over Jim's symptoms and blood test findings. He explained the medications to be used to replace the now low production of adrenal hormones, plans for improved nutrition, and other cares. Moritz stopped talking several times to ask Rita if she understood or had any questions.

When he had finished, Rita said: "Well, considering the overall picture of Jim's condition and future, I guess these latest studies could have been worse."

Moritz took another drink of his tea and Rita sipped on her wine. There was an extended pause in their conversation.

Finally, Rita spoke: "Victor, can I call you Victor? I really need to talk to you about several things that I have been holding in and not sharing with anyone."

Victor said: "Of course, Rita, tell me what's on your mind." He moved his position on the sofa to make it easier to look directly into her eyes as she began speaking.

Rita said: "First of all, I have had a lot of frustration with Jim's progress. First good news and remission with treatments, then relapse and the cancer reappears with vengeance and metastases. More treatments and remission, then relapse again. How many times did we go up and down, it's hard to remember sometimes?"

"I did have mixed feelings when we were given

the news of more trouble this morning. Then Jim made his decision to continue trying, after we talked it over. He really wants to live to make it into your study, and I will support him for better or worse. I am not blaming you for the way things have gone for Jim. I know that this roller coaster scene often happens with all kinds of cancers. I am just telling you how frustrating it can be as it goes on and on."

Rita paused, then continued before Victor could respond: "I also have really deep guilt feelings that I cannot do more, or have not done enough, to help Jim get better. I try to make him comfortable to lessen his pain, but the pain does not really go away. I try to help him be more mobile, but he is getting weaker and frailer each week it seems. I feel guilty that I have not been able to improve his nutrition and put some weight back on him. I know that he is suffering from cachexia. This is the cancer causing him not wanting to eat, and the muscle wasting. I know this happens in many cancer patients, but I still feel guilty about it. Now I know that some of Jim's nutrition and energy problems are in part due to this adrenal hemorrhage event. Still, maybe I could have done a better job of feeding Jim and watching his weight these last several weeks."

"Victor, a few times I have even thought that it would not be too bad if Jim didn't make it into your Nanoshpere study. That is awful of me, I know, because that means that he has no hope of surviving for much longer. By not encouraging him more positively to enter an experimental protocol, am I wishing his death to come sooner? That's a hell of a thing to wish on your husband who loves you. But, he is so miserable and in so much pain. It is all so confusing and depressing to me. I have even thought of asking someone to increase his pain medications to maybe shorten the number of days of his suffering. However, you know, that would be like assisting him in committing suicide. I really don't want to do that."

Rita then said with both despair and anger in her voice: "Sometimes I wish this damn Nanosphere study would fail approval before Jim is subjected to any more hopeful thinking. Then he would just give up."

By this time, Rita had finished her second glass of wine. Victor Moritz had also finished his tea. Victor had listened intently to Rita's venting her frustrations and guilt over Jim's terminal condition. Yet, she was in part, holding out hope for his recovery. Moritz remained quiet, waiting to see if Rita had more to say.

***

After pausing for a minute or so, Rita said: "I am going to the kitchen for a cup of coffee and then come back to continue this awful confession. I will bring you some more hot water for your tea."

On her way to the kitchen Rita reached out and gently touched Victor's shoulder and back of his neck. Moritz did not respond.

When Rita returned and sat Victor's tea water on the coffee table, she pulled her chair closer to his place on the sofa. They talked some about what Rita had said already. Victor told Rita that he understood why she had such concerns and feelings. He stressed to her that her feelings and concerns were very common in spouses and support persons of patients facing the situations that she and Jim were facing.

Moritz suggested that Rita meet with the cancer clinic's Social Worker and even consider trying psychotherapy to see if these interactions might help her deal with some of her feelings. Rita said she had thought of this previously, but never followed through with it. However, she promised Victor that she would try to meet with these resources sometime in the next couple weeks. Victor was not sure how serious Rita was about following through with this, but he continued to encourage her to make the commitment.

After finishing that discussion, Rita brought out another feeling she wanted to face Victor with: "Victor, as I am sure you know from your experience with many other patients, Jim's condition has essentially stopped our sexual interactions for more than two years."

Victor said: "Yes, Rita, this is almost a certain side effect of the extensive medication, radiation, and surgery that Jim has received treating his prostate cancer. I am sorry for this, and I wish we could do more to avoid these particular consequences, as well as others."

Rita continued: "Victor, I am still a relatively young woman with, thankfully, a healthy and sensitive body. I care for Jim as best as I can, consult with advice to the new bakery owners when they ask for it, then take care of our house and all else. Though busy, I still have unfulfilled physical and sexual desires. Lately, even sexual fantasies. To be specific, I have recently had fantasies of making love with you."

At this point, Rita left her chair and moved over to sit on the arm of the sofa beside Victor. She moved her thigh to touch his, and then turned and pressed her breasts to his shoulder as she put her hand on the back of his head and moved her lips toward his. Victor, surprised momentarily, felt her passion in this embrace, but he did not kiss Rita.

Rita held her embrace and whispered: "Please forgive me, Victor, but I have thought of touching you so often the last several weeks. I am craving closeness and the touch of a whole man. You are Jim's and my hero and I admire you so much. Then tonight, I could not resist this urge and opportunity to hold you."

She again pressed into his body and held tight for a moment. Rita then slid off the arm of the sofa to sit beside Victor and started to loosen his tie and unbutton his shirt.

Moritz finally realized how serious this was becoming. He gently, but firmly, took hold of Rita's hands to stop her from going further.

He said: "Rita. You are a beautiful, sensitive, and caring woman that any man would enjoy sharing the experience of making love with. I am sure it could be complete bliss. However, this cannot happen between us. You are under a heavy and almost unbearable stress dealing with Jim's illness and the effects of that on your relationship and your marriage."

"I realize, from what you have said this evening, that you have many difficult frustrations to face, try to handle and resolve. However, you would regret being unfaithful to Jim, even given all the reasons you have to rationalize the situation. You would have a difficult time forgiving yourself afterwards. As would I."

"Also, please realize that I have a responsibility to uphold the Oath of Hippocrates. This might sound old fashioned to you, but I swore to this Oath when I became a Physician. In our situation, the relevant part of that Oath is:

'Whatever houses I may visit, I will come for the benefit of the sick, remaining free of all intentional injustice, of all mischief and in particular of sexual relations with both female and male persons, be they free or slaves.'

As Victor spoke, Rita had begun checking her passion and let her hands fall back on her lap. Victor had released them from his firm but gentle grip that had restrained her.

He continued: "Also, Rita, I am in a serious faithful relationship with another woman who trusts that she and I are destined to spending the rest of our lives together, just as you and Jim are."

Rita was now sobbing, her face buried in her hands. After a minute or so, sitting more upright and wiping the tears, she said: "Victor, I am so sorry. Can you forgive me? I lost control of myself.

My fantasy attraction to you has been building for several months. After the accumulation of my guilt and frustration I told you about, Jim's new problem, seeing you at the clinic today, and then you coming by the house when I was alone, I let myself go."

By this time, Moritz had redone his tie and checked the button of his shirt. He stood up, reached out and took Rita's hand, helping her up from the sofa.

He said: "Rita, you do not need to apologize further. You are having a very rough time right now. I hope you accept that I was honest in my response to you. I hold no disrespect towards you, and I meant what I said about your beauty. I urge you to follow-up on my suggestion about seeing some of the clinic's support persons. For my part, I will not talk to anyone about what happened here tonight."

"Believe me Rita, I will continue to do my best to help Jim. He is lucky to have a spouse like you that loves and supports him."

Victor then put his arm around Rita's shoulder and they walked to the door together, parting with quietly spoken goodnights.

Dr. Victor Moritz drove straight home, thinking of today's unusual experience.

***

Moritz spent the following day at his desk in the laboratory preparing a lecture for the Regional Cancer Society meeting next month. He had been invited to present his recent research discoveries leading to his proposed clinical study using the Nanosphere Complex.

Friday morning he worked in his office preparing for the Committee meeting next week. That afternoon, Moritz cared for patients in the outpatient clinic.

Dr. Moritz had gone to the Oncology ward to check on Jim's progress each day. As the medications started to take effect, Jim's adrenal deficiency condition was improving. His blood coagulation factors continued to be normal, and there had been no further hemorrhage into the adrenal glands.

8

Saturday, and Victor Moritz awoke early. He was looking forward to Ruth's visit this weekend, her first time seeing his home and work site at Lake View. She was renting a car at the airport and he expected her arrival at about 10:00 AM this morning.

He generally kept his modest 1500 square foot cabin clean and in good order. This morning, however, he again cleaned and organized some in the bathroom, kitchen and the enclosed deck. Finishing that, he showered, dressed and ate breakfast. Before leaving, Victor exercised Shadow and put him back into the kennel. He then took a bucket of grain from the shed and emptied it into the feed bunker for the steers. They seemed to sense this daily event and he could hear their running towards the bunker through the early autumn morning's misty beginning, with traces of sunrise breaking through.

Dr. Moritz arrived at the Hospital at about 7:30 AM. At the Oncology ward, he stopped at the Nurses' station before visiting Jim. The Nurse in charge gave Dr. Moritz a brief summary of Jim's night. He had rested very well after some minimal sedation. His heart rate, blood pressure, blood oxygen level, and urine output had been stable and within normal limits for the last 24 hours. Jim was tolerating his medications without a problem. He seemed to have become better adjusted and resolved to accept his recent medical setback and sudden admission to the Hospital on Wednesday morning.

Moritz then logged onto the computer and reviewed the completed notes added to Jim's chart by others involved in his care since yesterday morning. This included a Respiratory Therapy assistant, the night Nurse, and the Resident Physician on call the past 12 hours. There was also a consult note from the Endocrinologist. His note supported Dr. Moritz's conclusions about the problem with Jim's adrenal glands, and his agreement with the present medication approach.

Jim was in a sitting position in the Hospital bed and watching TV, which he switched off when Dr. Moritz came into the room. After shaking hands and morning greetings, Moritz briefly examined Jim, listening to his heart and lungs, checking for leg edema, and gentle palpation of his abdomen. Jim gave some feedback about his feeling markedly improved, relative to when he was admitted on Wednesday. Dr. Moritz told Jim some of his blood laboratory test results from early this morning. These had again shown steady progress. He said possibly they would consider discharge Monday morning if things kept improving as trending thus far. The key word at this time was 'possibly'. Jim seemed satisfied with Dr. Moritz's assessment and thanked him.

Two days ago, on Thursday morning, Dr. Moritz told Jim about stopping at his home on Wednesday evening as Jim had requested. Moritz told Jim that he sat and talked with Rita for about an hour. He had reviewed with her Jim's illness, the recent setback, the additional medications and plans for getting him back home.

Moritz had told Jim it was obvious that Rita loved her husband and that she was being very strong and supportive during his illness. In addition, Moritz alerted Jim that he thought Rita was feeling an increased sense of despair, frustration, and maybe some depression. He said he thought that she was masking these feelings from Jim, and others. Moritz had suggested that she and Jim together start seeing the Oncology Social Worker and consider some psychotherapy to start exploring these questions. They should also consider starting a regular interaction with these services for a few weeks.

Jim had been thoughtful about what Moritz said and had responded: "Doc, I have been wondering myself about Rita's overwhelming anxiety, frustration, and possible depression for at least a couple of months now. We did meet once with your support team a year ago, but then we chose to go it alone, and not to return to them. However, I realize it is getting harder on Rita, and I think your suggestion is a good one." Jim then told Moritz that he would talk with Rita about this issue soon. Moritz and Jim did not discuss this issue again on Friday morning nor today.

Now, after this morning's evaluation and review with Jim about his progress, Moritz said: "Jim, my associate, Dr. Cooper, will be looking in on you tomorrow morning. Do you have any more questions or concerns that I can help with today?"

Jim paused, then smiling, said: "Dr. Victor Moritz, go have a good weekend. The Nurses told me that your girlfriend was coming to town today, so the word is out. Rita will be visiting me this afternoon and I will tell her about a possible release from here on Monday."

With that, Moritz and Jim gave each other a thumbs-up as Moritz was leaving the room.

Dr. Moritz added Jim's progress notes into the computer records, spoke with the Nurse and Medical Resident briefly about Jim's condition, and left the Hospital.

When Moritz pulled into his driveway, he saw a car parked by the cabin. The steers were also up by the shed, expecting another bucket of feed. Shadow was standing beside Ruth, who was waving towards his car.

Victor and Ruth moved quickly to be wrapped by each other's arms in a full body embrace. They kissed, took a breath and kissed again. Then Shadow wanted in the act and he started nosing his way between them. Victor eased his embrace of Ruth and said: "Ruth, it is great to see you. Thanks so much for coming."

Ruth, kissing him again on the cheek and squeezing his arm said: "Vic, I have missed you very much. I think I love you."

Victor responded: "Ruth, I certainly love you as well! Let's enjoy a couple of days together! Let me help you get your bags inside and then I can start showing you around the place. The cabin is rather small, but we have 40 acres to see."

They entered the cabin's South entrance through the screened deck and then into the great room. The kitchen was to the right, with windows facing East and South. Straight ahead, at the back and middle of the great room space, was a stone hearth containing a free standing wood burning stove, behind which was a flat stone wall the width of the hearth. Victor led Ruth past the hearth into a hallway that had a bedroom on each end of the cabin, and a central bathroom. The East end of the hallway ended with a utility space, washer and drier and an exit to the attached garage.

Victor said, putting his arm around her waist after setting down the travel luggage in the West bedroom: "Ruth, you can unpack and spread out your things in this bedroom and feel it is your own. But to tell you the truth, I hope we are sleeping together in my bedroom at the other end of the hall."

Ruth turned, hugged Victor and said: "I accept both of those terms with pleasure and anticipation."

While Ruth was unpacking, freshening up, and getting into some comfortable slacks and shirt, Victor went to the kitchen. He prepared a snack tray of cheese, rye bread, olives and some slices of various fruits. He asked Ruth if she preferred coffee or wine for this lunch-snack. She said that coffee would be great at this time. He put on a pot of coffee and heated water for some tea for himself. He then took the snacks, a couple of small plates and eating utensils out onto the table of the screened deck. In another few minutes, the coffee and tea were ready, and he poured when Ruth had changed and stopped at the kitchen.

Victor said to Ruth: "Let's take our cups with us while I show you the rest of the house, or cabin as I usually call it."

Ruth, sipped from her coffee cup, touched Victor on the arm, and said: "I would like that."

Victor then showed Ruth his small study on the West side of the cabin, whose door opened to the great room. There were study windows facing West showing woods sloping up a hillside. He realized the entryway area on the East, which included the laundry and mud room, would be even less interesting to Ruth, but he showed them to her anyway. The kitchen, fully open to the great room, had modern appliances. The windows over the appliances and the work counters faced East and South to maximize sun exposure in the morning and winters. There was a multipurpose island and a modest sized table with 4 chairs in this kitchen area.

After some catching up conversation and eating a snack, Victor and Ruth put on hiking shoes, light jackets and hats, and started out for a walk through the property, accompanied by a free roaming Shadow. Two 5-6 acre pastures were adjacent to and West of the driveway.

On the East side of the driveway were the flower and vegetable gardens near the house and garage. Also, lining the driveway on the East was the beginnings of a small orchard. Thus far, the orchard consisted of a few semi-dwarf apple trees of various sizes, species and age, and two cherry trees. Most were done fruiting for this year. Victor told Ruth he picked and ate fresh apples, took some to give to hospital and lab workers, and laid some aside for eating into the Fall and Winter. Of the few cherries produced thus far, he had eaten some fresh. With others, he had made an effort in canning a couple half pints. That had seemed like a lot of work, and he wasn't sure about doing it in the future.

Victor briefly showed Ruth the outbuildings for the cattle and the machine shed. Victor and Ruth then walked to the hilly woodland that was behind the cabin and buildings. They hiked side by side where the trail had been widened by Victor's efforts in his spare time and for some exercise. Otherwise, only a narrow, yet obvious, course of a deer path was evident. This trail allowed an approach up to the ridge that ran along the property line. After hiking up to the ridge, they took a break, setting on the stump of a fallen oak tree.

They talked almost constantly during the hike. Ruth had shared some of her work experiences, both rewarding and some that were frustrating. Victor had briefly reviewed with Ruth the status of his clinical research study, the Committee meeting and Jim's condition. He talked about his friend Otto Zellers, especially how much he liked Otto's friendship. Victor also remarked how, in many ways, Otto reminded him of his own father, now passed. Both his father and Otto had grown as children during the Great Depression and had experienced many similar family hardships and losses during WW II.

After their break, Victor and Ruth hiked the ridge, enjoying the view of the cabin and surroundings, a few hundred feet below. The downhill trail led back to the gardens by the cabin. Then they embraced, telling each other how nice it was to be able to hike and see one another again.

***

Ruth and Victor took turns using the bathroom and shower. When they met in the kitchen afterwards, Victor had already started barbecue coals on the deck, and also a small fire in the wood stove of the Great Room, as the early evening was beginning to cool. They shared preparing chunks of chicken and garden vegetables for cooking at the grill. After these were ready, they moved the food to a table in front of the wood burning stove and positioned a sofa for sitting. Water and wine were enjoyed with their food.

The first several minutes and bites of food were satisfying for each without much talking. They just delighted in the atmosphere and this time together. As they relaxed more, eating became less hasty and conversation began again. Ruth complimented Victor on his home and property. They talked again of how they enjoyed the hiking together today.

With this talk of hiking, Victor said: "You know, Ruth, three out of four times when we have been together, we have done some pretty serious hiking – Grays Peak, Camelback, and the Grand Canyon. Even today, though not a mountain, we did some hiking work and saw some decent scenery that wasn't concrete pavement, shopping malls, or housing developments."

"Have you ever thought of this? Would exploring the outdoors and visiting more of our country's National Parks and Monuments be part of our life style if we lived together? What would you or I be willing to do to live near mountains or a forest wilderness? What feelings do you have when seeing, experiencing, or just being near, mountains or other unique landscapes that have awesome scenery?"

Ruth thought for a moment, then said: "Oh Vic, yes I have often thought about our hike outings together. Here is the way I feel right now. I would change jobs, I would move to another state, and change other things within my power if necessary, to participate with you in more of the things you are describing. I am sure the feelings I have right now are, in part, the result of just being with you, as a person I now love. But, to be sure, I purely enjoy a challenge and experiences of the outdoors, a hike, climb, or special view."

Ruth took another swallow of her wine and then said: "Vic, now let me turn the last part of your questions back on you. What are some of the feelings you have when experiencing a mountain or other sights you are talking about?"

Now it was Victor's turn to take a drink of wine, then he said: "Ruth, the feelings I have when hiking a mountain, a canyon, a forest, or enjoying other similar displays of our Earth's natural wonders, are hard to clearly or easily explain. It is probably different for each person. However, I will try to tell you about some of my feelings and thoughts with such experiences."

"I visited Rocky Mountain National Park a few weeks after my Father died. I hiked some trails to the higher elevations, took my time and enjoyed many great views. During that time, I felt that the higher elevation and effort had brought me closer to his spirit, if there are such things as a spirit, or a God. Maybe I was just feeling remorseful about my father's death, but I experienced that feeling."

***

"I wondered, is there communication with cherished ones after their passing? Many people believe they will be with their spouse after death. Some say they are not afraid of death because they will see their loved one again. Lots of mankind believe in a God and a life after passing from Earth. This has occurred in most civilizations on our planet, it seems, and there is much evidence of worshiping a higher power in many past and present cultures."

"On the other hand, there are agnostic and atheist views. One can say science has not proven a God or Spirit communication. However, is scientific proof possible or necessary? Science has not yet discovered or explained many other things around us or in the Universe. Science is the product of human efforts, so how can it find the

Creator, if there is one? But Ruth, I am getting in way over my head with this discussion. I'm just saying, I had that closeness feeling when taking that hike in Rocky Mountain National Park. Like I said, maybe it was just simple thinking over a lot of memories of Dad at the time."

Ruth moved closer to Victor. She was looking straight into his eyes and said: "Vic, please go on."

Victor then said: "OK, dear Ruth, you asked for it. I have a few times climbed a moderate mountain, finishing by essentially crawling up a final slope of chunks of stone, after making it through a snow field during the ascent, then reaching a summit. The panoramic views one sees, not only from the summit but also many times during the ascent, are visually astounding. Often there is serenity to enjoy. Sometimes nature puts on a show with storms over the range, which continues for miles before your eyes. It is hard to describe the great beauty. Maybe that is why almost everyone is taking pictures, to remind themselves of being there, as well as to help them attempt to describe the experience to others."

"Such an occurrence makes me realize my smallness in the face of the Earth's mass. Also, such experiences make me humble, because my small speck occurs in a very tiny length of time, compared to Earth's age, let alone the Universe. So, to say it again, these experiences make me feel, at that time, in harmony with Earth, and also make me feel very meek and humble."

"I do not need the act of actually standing on a mountain summit as an absolute necessity to feel this way. Just being in the foothills, or encountering many other of nature's wonders, a canyon, forest, seashore, a great prairie and others can ignite these feelings."

Victor then took a break and refilled his and Ruth's empty wine glasses. Returning from the kitchen, he bent over and kissed her ear and gave her a brief massage of the back of her neck and shoulders.

When he resumed his seat beside Ruth, he said: "Now, my final confessions on this topic tonight. So, I feel humbled and am only a small dot on Earth and in human's course through time. But, I am a definite part of it. Being so, my question is, how should I live?"

"I feel the way for me to make the most of my short existence is to seek happiness and be productive. I am trying to obtain happiness and achievement by using a rational mind, respect for myself and others, and honest hard work. This could, in some small way, be a plus for Mother

Earth."

Victor paused with a smile. Then he said: "Yes, I realize cancer is still so devastating to mankind, and not yet beaten. Yet, I feel happiness and satisfaction that my career efforts might contribute some useful knowledge to the field of cancer biology."

"So, Ruth, this was an attempt to say what I experience in my mind oftentimes when out in Nature. I hope to enjoy more of Nature as my life goes on. I have not seen that much of our planet. However, I believe that if and when I do see and experience more, I will have similar feelings to those that I have just tried to express to you. Let's try to enjoy some of these experiences together if we can. Hope I didn't bore you with this ranting, dear Ruth."

Then Victor said: "How about let's go to bed?

Ruth said: "Vic, this is a great idea."

They cleared the dishes and left over food from the table by the hearth and cleaned things in the kitchen. Ruth went to change while Victor refilled the wood stove for one more burn of the evening. He let Shadow out briefly and back in, then make sure the doors were secured. He checked for phone messages. Thankfully, there were none.

After Ruth was finished, Victor took his turn in

the bathroom and changing. Ruth then joined him in his bedroom. They made love passionately, and talked afterwards about their relationship. Eventually, Ruth turned on her left side, Victor snuggled up to her back, put his arm around her, and they dozed off into a satisfying night of sleep.

9

At breakfast in the morning, Victor and Ruth talked about what they might do today. Another hike and mountain feelings were off the table. Ruth said she would like to see some of Victor's work place. She expressed interest in seeing the inside of his research laboratory, the outpatient clinic part of the hospital, and general layout of the buildings of the Medical Center. They agreed they should not visit any of his hospitalized patients. One reason was that Ruth saw patients every day at her own job. The other reason was out of respect for Victor's patients' privacy. Most were ill with different stages of their cancer and many likely would already have family and friends visiting today, a Sunday. Finally, Victor had already had Dr. Cooper seeing his patients this morning for their medical care.

Victor mentioned that his good friend, Otto Zellers, had wanted to meet Ruth when she came to visit. Ruth was all for this, so Victor called Otto and asked him if they could drop by his place in the afternoon, not for lunch, just a short visit. This was fine with Otto.

When they left the cabin, the sun was shining on a cool autumn day, and the leaves were near full color. They drove to the Lake View Medical Center and parked in a lot at the Research Laboratory Building, which was near, but separate from the Hospital itself. At an entrance of this 4 story Research Building, Victor scanned his Medical Faculty ID card and they entered the building's atrium.

A hallway led to the elevators which they took to the 2nd floor where Victor's laboratory was, among the other research laboratories on each side of the hallway. Victor showed Ruth some of the rooms centrally located on the floor that were shared use spaces. Ruth was not very interested in the special instrument equipment or refrigeration rooms. She was more inquisitive about the facilities for procedures such as cell isolation.

The door to Dr. Moritz's lab was closed, but not locked. Lights were on suggesting someone was there, which concerned Victor for a moment. He was relieved to see two of his research team working at their lab benches. One was the Graduate Student, Mark, and the other was Charlie, a Medical Student. Each greeted Dr. Moritz as he entered the lab. He, in turn, promptly introduced each to Ruth. Moritz suggested that Mark and Charlie spend a couple minutes briefly telling Ruth what their individual work was, and how it related and fit into the laboratory's overall research goals.

After they had finished, Ruth asked Mark and Charlie to also tell her something about themselves. She did this in part to be polite. She also hoped to learn more about the type of person Victor had selected to work with his research program.

Mark spoke up first. Mark and his wife had a two year old son. His wife, Susan, was working in the nearby community at a flower shop. Mark, 27 years old, was in his 4th year of Graduate School training and research with Dr. Moritz. He hoped to complete his work and receive a PhD. this year. Mark often put in 60 hours a week research activity in the lab and had been taking one course each semester that was required to obtain his degree. He sometimes helped his wife in the evening with their son, as often as he could manage getting some free time. He seemed honest, respectful and was obviously a hard worker.

Charlie was 26 years old and in his 4th year of Medical School. Charlie was voluntarily working a few hours a week in Moritz's lab this year. He wanted to specialize in Oncology after his 3 years of Pediatric Residency. He had selected to spend time in Dr. Moritz's lab specifically because he thought Moritz was an excellent role model for his own future professional plans. His plans were to complete a Postdoctoral Fellowship in Oncology and start a career in Oncology clinical care and research. Charlie's work experience in Moritz's lab would help him obtain a Postdoctoral Fellowship training appointment at a University with a strong Oncology program. Charlie's wife was a Nurse working in one of Lake View's outpatient clinics. Ruth was impressed by Charlie's rational approach and plan to obtain his goals. She also noted that Charlie had confidence that he would achieve them.

After this brief interaction with Mark and Charlie, Victor showed Ruth some laboratory equipment, giving a short description of the function of some of the specialized instruments. A few minutes later, after a short tour around the lab bench spaces and Victor and Dr. Li Chen's office, they said goodbye to Mark and Charlie.

Leaving the lab, Victor told Ruth how grateful he was for the work of Mark, Charlie and Dr. Chen. He then explained that all 4 floors of the building were arranged similar to those on the 2nd floor where they were.

Next they took the elevator back to the ground floor. After exiting the building, they followed a sidewalk to a door that was the back entrance to the outpatient clinic of the Hospital building. Here they looked at examples of a typical waiting room area, patient examining rooms, procedure and treatment rooms, small conference rooms, and physician and staff offices.

The outpatient space ended at a reception and registration area. Down another hallway was the start of the Emergency Care facility. Victor and Ruth did not enter the Emergency Care area. It extended to and was contingent with one wing of the inpatient rooms of the Hospital.

Instead, they exited into an open yard and flower garden that was enclosed by various shrubbery plantings. This space was available to all employees of the Medical Center as a place to take a break and get a bit of fresh air. The area was also open to patients that were mobile on their own, or in wheel chairs, and had permission from their Physician.

Ruth and Victor sat on one of the benches in this area and Victor pointed out different parts of the inpatient hospital building to Ruth, explaining the six different floors, facilities contained in them and how they interacted. After this, they walked back to the small food court, which was on the first floor of the Hospital building, to have lunch.

***

During the drive to Otto's home, Victor gave Ruth some insight about his friendship with this man. Otto had been a Family Practice physician for 40 years and often tutored Medical Residents from Lake View at his clinic. Victor told Ruth how he and Otto became good friends while Otto was a volunteer in patient case discussions with Medical Students for the past several years, a program that Victor also regularly participated in.   A solid friendship occurred when they found they held similar views on other topics besides medicine, even politics.

Otto had seen them arrive in his driveway and had opened the door already by the time Ruth and Victor reached the steps on his porch.

Otto said: "Welcome to both of you."

Victor introduced Ruth as they entered the house.

Otto suggested: "Have a seat anywhere. The coffee pot is on and hot tea water as well if you are interested in either."

Tea was preferred by all three, so they made their way to the kitchen, selected a tea bag, poured their cup, and returned to chairs in the living room. Otto brought in a small plate of bakery made sugar cookies and placed them on the coffee table near everyone's chair.

Ruth gave Otto a brief summary of her past, having a Registered Nurse and Master's degrees, and now working as a Nurse Practitioner on the Pediatric cancer ward in the Phoenix Children's Hospital. She briefly covered how she had met Victor and spoke a little about their communications since then.

To get Ruth off the hook for a while, Victor changed the conversation towards Otto. Otto said he was feeling pretty much the same as he was a few days ago when Victor had visited. Otto commented on the beautiful fall weather and told them how he was starting to clean off his garden before winter set in.

Otto asked Victor if he was worried about the next Committee meeting. Victor said he thought he would be able to still make a good case for his study, but didn't discuss too many specifics. He brushed off talking about too many details or worries. Mostly, he did not want Ruth to feel that her visit was interfering with time he needed to be spending on preparation for the Committee on Tuesday.

Otto thought for a moment, then said: "I wish you both continued success in what you are doing in medicine and nursing. Much of health care has really changed in the last few years. Take for example, a simple thing like charting and record keeping mechanisms that are current now. I had a rough time learning how to enter material into the computer record, and get information out, as the Hospitals were changing over to these new computer methods. But I eventually learned it. I hope these changes continue to be improved and that the cost is justified. We need to monitor if there is improved overall hospital and medical care, less iatrogenic errors, and improved patient outcomes. Objectively assessed of course. You should keep your eyes open in evaluating many of these new changes. Just don't swallow them whole. I could talk on about other things such as the increased role of government, tort reform, just fee for service, etc."

Otto then suddenly changed his oratory: "But, hey, I am sorry to go off on these kind of issues on such a nice day, especially on such a fine event as meeting you, Ruth. I don't know what you two are planning with your relationship, but I hope the best for you both."

After several more minutes of the three talking, Victor suggested that he and Ruth should get back to the cabin. Otto did not put up much resistance. He maybe was a little embarrassed for tangentially politicizing some of the conversation. Also, it was getting late in the afternoon. By this time of day, he usually started to feel tired and needed a little rest for himself. He and Ruth joined in a sincere hug before parting, each saying how good it was to meet each other. Otto and Victor had a firm handshake. Then Ruth and Victor left Otto's home.

***

The drive to Victor's cabin was pretty quiet. Ruth had said what a good experience it was to meet Otto. He was obviously one of Victor's most cherished friends. Both Victor and Ruth were feeling a little down, realizing how fast the weekend had gone, and that already this was their last evening together for some time. When they arrived back at Victor's, Shadow was jumping in his kennel and looking forward to being let out to run freely for a while.

It now was late afternoon. Ruth played retrieve the ball with Shadow while Victor took feed to the steers. A light breeze was bringing down some tree leaves and the day was cooling off. On the porch, before going inside, Ruth and Victor hugged, kissed, and expressed to each other how great the time spent together had been.

Inside, Victor washed up and headed for the

kitchen, and Ruth went to shower and start packing to leave early in the morning. Victor started BBQ coals and prepared chicken and vegetable chunks onto skewers. He opened a bottle of wine and poured two glasses, waiting for Ruth to join him before sipping from his own. Loaded skewers, wine and a dessert of cheesecake that Victor had purchased on Friday would be their meal this evening. Not much different than last night, but satisfying.

By the time Ruth had refreshed herself and packed some of her things, Victor had started a fire in the Great Room's wood burning stove and put on a CD of light classical music of Mozart. They sat on the couch by the stove, relaxed and sipped their wine, listening to the music for a few minutes, each absorbed in their own thoughts.

When the skewers were finished over the coals, Victor brought them into the kitchen. He and Ruth each filled a plate, and went back to sit and eat near the warming stove. Shadow, a model of obedience, stayed on his padded spot by the door leading to the deck.

Ruth and Victor satisfied their hunger, but did not stuff themselves. During the meal, they talked some of how each was viewing their relationship.

Victor, clearing his throat, said: "Ruth, I would

like to ask you to marry me, but before doing so, I think I should be more settled in my career objectives and location. The situation with my clinical study with Nanosphere targeting metastases idea seems so controversial at Lake View at the present. I am considering, win or lose with the approval process, that I might look for another cancer Research Center to go forward with my career."

After a pause and taking Ruth's hand, he continued: "Would you consider marrying me, not right now, but sometime in the not too distant future? Is it insulting to you that I suggest waiting for me to settle these things at Lake View?"

Ruth touched his arm, and said: "Yes Vic, I am sure I will marry you when you actually ask. To tell the truth, however, I agree it is best if you settle and solve the concerns you have about your research project, Lake View, and a possible move. Let's work these and a few other things through before we marry."

"Vic, thinking now before marriage, we also have some questions of mine to talk about. For example, what are your attitudes about having children? I am now 33 years old and would want to seriously consider having children. Another question, will you be at home together with me a reasonable amount of time, and not be consumed by your career objectives to the exclusion of time for us? You are a driven man for achievement, you know."

"Will the possibility of my wanting to continue to work be discussed if you look for another job? I might want to consider continuing my own career in Nursing. So, it might matter to me where you are looking to relocate. Would there be job opportunities at this new site for me to work as well? I don't mean to fight you on these questions, Vic, I am just saying we have several issues to discuss as we go forward."

Victor said: "Ruth, I am so glad you spoke up about these things. Yes Ruth, our love and a mutual respect for the independence of each other will not be at risk of failure. We can have a great time working on these decisions together."

Ruth spoke again: "Vic, this visit here with you has encouraged me to trust you more on many of these issues. You do take time for something besides your professional work. Your interest and care of your home, with attention to its responsibilities and respect for your land have shown me that you do take some time off away from the lab and Hospital. I have noticed other things as well. Your sensitivity and friendship with

Otto. Your concern about patients, like Jim is another example. The people you have in your research program seem genuine. These impressions on me go a long way in showing your good will towards others."

"You love being outdoors and are thoughtful when experiencing it. Enjoying mountain climbs, other nature hikes, views and experiences, working in the earth with your hands in the garden, orchard, and the path in your woods are other things of importance. The thoughts and feelings you told me yesterday show me how you are reflecting on things, maybe even about the way man should live."

Ruth continued: "I know these are only brief glimpses of your total personality and being, but they seem true to me and speak very well of you."

Ruth then said: "So Vic, I see all things heading in the right direction for us. It sounds like we will get together after a little more time working on it. Let's go forward in nurturing our love, commitment and compromises."

Vic moved closer to Ruth on the sofa, took her hand and gave it a gentle squeeze, saying: "Ruth, I am so glad we started this discussion. I have been thinking about it for weeks, and wondering what your thoughts were. Let's please keep up this conversation, certainly even after you get back to Phoenix, Okay?"

Ruth nodded yes and squeezed his hand back. Vic then said: "Ruth, it's getting late and you have an hour's drive in the morning to make your early flight. How about I clean up the kitchen stuff while you finish your packing, then we meet in my bedroom?"

Ruth winked and softly said: "Yes." She gave him a nudge in his side with her elbow, and headed to pack and freshen up for bed.

***

After meeting in Vic's bedroom, they began slowly undressing each other. Ruth, although being five feet seven inches tall, still had to reach up to remove Vic's pajama top from the shoulders of his six foot two frame. After removing Ruth's pajama blouse, Vic laid his hands high on her chest, just below her neckline. He then moved them slowly and rhythmically down her breasts to her now erected nipples, which he rolled gently in his fingertips. Her eyes were closed and her head and shoulders arched back slightly, enjoying the touches he was giving her.

Ruth responded by placing her hands on Vic's abdomen and moving them up to his chest, scratching lightly until reaching his responding nipples as well. Then urgently, they embraced and kissed each other while holding their bodies as close as possible, his erection and her passion obvious. Vic's hands held Ruth's hips as he pressed her to him. Ruth caressed back while moving her breasts against his chest.

After dropping their pajama bottoms, Vic took Ruth in his arms, and rolled both over onto the bed, with her body under his. Ruth gasped softly with satisfaction as Vic slowly and gently entered her moist vagina. They continued to make love, altering their positions, until both had complete physical and verbal explosive climaxes.

They kissed, snuggled against each other, and soon were sound asleep.

Fortunately, Vic had set the alarm for 5:00 AM, so they awoke in time to have a cup of coffee and a good embrace and kiss. Ruth then used the bathroom, finished packing her toothbrush and cosmetics kit, and was ready, though reluctant, to be on the road for the drive to the Regional Airport. Vic was also obviously sad to see her leave. However, they had made arrangements for him to spend a weekend with her in Phoenix in two months.

Ruth gave Shadow a pat on the head and a neck

scratching on her way out the door. Vic carried her two bags and placed them in the car. They hugged, kissed, expressed their love for each other, and then had to part. Ruth drove slowly out the driveway, watching Vic waving in the car's rear view mirror.

10

Victor Moritz's education after High School started at a Midwest Liberal Arts college of less than 2000 students. He had an early interest in Biology and Chemistry, studied hard and maintained a high grade point average over the 4 years. In addition, he had worked 20 hours per week for a house building contractor, doing menial but necessary jobs, most requiring a pick and shovel or carrying lumber and cement blocks for the carpenter and stone mason. A pay check every two weeks helped relieve some of the expenses for college that his parents were otherwise paying.

During this undergraduate education, Victor realized that he wanted to explore further some of the interactions between Biology and Chemistry. He therefore applied to several graduate schools that offered a degree in Biochemistry. Victor was accepted as a Graduate Student in the Biochemistry Department of a newly started Medical School in the South-East United States. At first, Victor was a little over confident about his ambition and study habits. This led to some embarrassing grades on his first examinations as a Graduate Student. However, he responded to this temporary shake-up of his confidence by increasing his focus and efforts on the classroom material.

Victor especially enjoyed two educational activities during the Graduate School experience. One was tutoring students that needed some guidance while taking the Biochemistry course that was required for all Medical Students. Victor liked this opportunity of relating to these students. While challenged by certain aspects of the Biochemistry course, all were clearly motivated to learn. They realized these basic science facts were the foundation of many aspects of the practice of medicine and understanding disease processes.

Another part of Graduate School that Victor also enjoyed was a research project of his own, which was required for a degree. Although subject to his faculty mentor's approval, Victor was expected to design and carry out experiments that objectively assessed hypotheses that he proposed. The goal of such a laboratory research experience was to develop an original idea or observation and scientifically prove it as factual. The results then could be written and published in a science journal for others to critique, learn from, or challenge.

Much of what Victor was learning in basic research appeared to him so obviously important in understanding the origins, symptoms, and treatments of many diseases encountered in the practice of Medicine. Thus, after receiving his PhD.

in Biochemistry, Victor applied to, and was accepted into Medical School. This was followed by a Residency in adult medicine and a Post-Doctoral Fellowship in Oncology.

So, 14 years after finishing his undergraduate College experience, Victor became a board certified adult medicine Oncologist. He chose to accept a position at The Ohio State School of Medicine. This Academic Medicine appointment gave him the opportunity to teach and relate to medical trainees at all levels of their education. Additionally, he was a part of a Department of Adult Oncology, and thus had a responsibility of direct clinical patient care. Finally, his appointment also left room of about a 20-25% of his time for the opportunity to pursue research. He designed hypotheses, obtained financial support for, and started basic research on cancer.

***

After seeing Ruth off this morning, Moritz had gone to his laboratory and reviewed with Dr. Chen the latest data she, Mark and Charlie had accumulated since talking together last Friday. This material was mainly complimentary data that supported a couple of points Moritz had made at the Committee meeting last week.

Moritz then left the laboratory and arrived at the Hospital's Oncology patient ward for Rounds at 9:00 AM. On Rounds, Moritz and the Oncology team would see and evaluate each of his patients. The team consisted of Moritz, Oncology Residents, Medical Students and a Nurse from the Oncology ward.

Presently, Dr. Moritz had 8 patients on the ward. At each patient's bedside, a Resident or Medical Student would present a brief history of the patient's illness, recent laboratory data, and other relevant information to Dr. Moritz and the rest of the Oncology team. Moritz would speak directly with each patient about how they were feeling, and ask if they had any questions that he might answer at that time. He also spent a few minutes performing a relevant physical examination. Earlier this morning, the Oncology Resident and Medical Student had already also carried out their own extensive physical examination on the patients as well.

Moritz would ask questions directed at the Medical team, to clarify issues or concerns he might have. After considering the type of answer, he would agree with the answer, or he would explain, clarify, and teach the team about this certain point. Depending on the patient's diagnosis, complications, progress, and laboratory studies, different patients required various amounts of time. When needed, further discussion and teaching points were made out in the hall as Moritz and the team moved to their next patient's room.

Jim was sitting up and Rita was beside him on the bed, holding hands and talking together when the team came into Jim's room. The medications that Jim was now receiving, which were replacing his adrenal glands' hormones, were producing satisfactory results. Blood pressure and daily urine production were in the normal range. Jim's mood and apparent strength seemed somewhat better. Laboratory results were also in the normal range today. After Dr. Moritz had examined Jim, he reviewed all the updated information with Jim and Rita. He asked the Resident and other team members if they thought Jim was stable enough to go home today.

Jim and Rita anxiously listened to the discussion between Dr. Moritz and the others. The consensus was that, yes, Jim was stable enough to be followed as an outpatient again, so discharge today was appropriate. Moritz then let the Resident summarize with Jim and Rita the laboratory and radiographic studies that would be obtained next week when Jim returned to be evaluated in the outpatient clinic. Moritz agreed with the Resident's summary. He then asked Jim and Rita if they were clear on this plan and if they had any other questions for him at this time.

Jim said: "Doc, I know I am not cured, but I do feel much better than a few days ago. I appreciate the fact that I can get back to our home, and see how it goes. I would like to shake everyone's hand in expressing my thanks, before you leave the room. As Jim was shaking everyone's hand, Rita was standing next to his bed and participated in this good news by giving everyone a verbal 'thank you' and a brief hug, including Victor Moritz.

The Oncology team finished seeing patients in about two and a half hours. Next, Dr. Moritz entered his notes on the patients into their computer records. The other members of the team worked on finishing up decisions and orders that Moritz had left up to them to complete, since they had discussed such items together on Rounds.

***

After completing his computer entries, Dr. Moritz got a quick sandwich from the Hospital deli and headed for his next meeting. Once every month, Moritz leads an early afternoon roundtable discussion with Residents and Medical Students. Their attendance was not required each month, but encouraged. Residents and Students working on other wards in Lake View Hospital were also invited, so the group was not exclusively Oncology trainees.

The objective of these sessions was to allow trainees and students the opportunity to bring up tangent questions on issues related to their profession. Usually the meetings were not focused on a particular patient or disease. Instead, the emphasis was on broader issues that had come up during their training that they wanted to hear discussed with their peers, as well as Faculty input. Other Faculty members sometimes attended and contributed comments.

When Moritz arrived at the conference room today, it was already nearly full, with over 30 persons. Several also had brought their lunch sandwiches and coffee. Moritz settled into one of the open chairs at the table, which had a circular arrangement so that everyone could clearly see one another.

At five minutes after the hour, he stood up and cleared his throat to help get the attention of the group.

Dr. Moritz said: "OK everyone, here we are at

our monthly discussion of issues that you have concerns about with respect to your career in Medicine. Does anyone have a concern or topic to bring up to start off? Speak freely now, you are not going to be graded for your participation if you do decide to add something to the discussion."

He then returned to his chair and looked around at the group while opening his sandwich wrapper. Most of the group were looking at each other for someone to start.

A 2nd year Resident, Emma, from the impatient Geriatric ward raised her hand to speak. She said: "Working on our Geriatric ward, I see the many different changes that age can bring to the human mind and body. Then recently, I read an article in a Medical Journal about the aging of Physicians in the United States. The data that concerned me was that 26% of Physicians in 2012 were over 60 years old, and this was expected to keep rising. Supportive numbers I looked up on the Internet showed that the percent of Physicians greater than 65 years old has risen from 17.8% in 2000 to 21.5% in 2011. This worries me so I thought I would bring it up for discussion."

Dr. Moritz said: "Thank you Emma for launching our session with an interesting observation. I am thinking of two questions regarding this issue. The first I will ask you to comment on since you raised the issue, and the second I will ask later to the rest of our group for discussion. Emma, what are your concerns about aging physicians?"

Emma thought for a bit, then said: "I have seen much with my patients on the Geriatric ward. With aging, very often there is a change in motor and cognitive function, decreasing from their usual levels. This change may only be subtle and not grossly recognized. So, I worry about safe and competent health care from aging Physicians that might be affected by their age. I know that older Physicians can bring valuable clinical expertise from their years of medical practice and this is very important. However, I am concerned, and support I guess, that our older Physicians' competency should be evaluated by some criteria, maybe even mandatory and on a regular basis. This evaluation might then be used to support or limit their practice of Medicine."

Dr. Moritz asked if anyone in the room had any ideas on how competency of aging Physicians could be assessed, or what variables might affect getting a rational and objective answer.

Jack, a 4th year Medical Student raised his hand and asked to speak: "It seems to me that some basic data could be assessed. For example, the mortality rate, hospital re-admission rate, complications, and so forth in patients of a Physician are already in a data base. These could be obtained from Clinic and Hospital records. Regarding cognitive dysfunction, tests and methods to recognize this are well established, and could be used as they are for the general aging population."

Hank, the Chief Resident of the Internal Medicine service, was next to contribute: "I see serious problems with subjecting a Physician to a special performance inquiry just because of age. Is the competency judgement going to be a Hospital credentialing responsibility, or a license renewal requirement after age 60 or 65 or 70? Or is this evaluation coming from a National mandate, like so many government regulations coming out these days? Any performance assessments will require new levels of oversight personal, accompanied by increased expense in dollars. Also, there will be extra anxiety and a stigma that these Physicians will experience. Most Physicians are members of Hospital staffs, and there are already in place patient practice committees that evaluate questionable cares by any Physician."

"I see, depending on the competency testing and guidelines established, a potential infringement on the individual rights of the Physician to make their own decision on when to take down their shingle. I see possible flaws in the assessment tools. My gut feeling is that a perceived decline in physical or cognitive function of medical practice skills does not change at the same rate or same degree in all aging Physicians. Their location of practice, isolated, rural, distance to available subspecialties or Hospital services, solo or large group practices, can have an impact on some of any supposedly objective criteria of performance by the aging Physician. These factors might affect any Physician for that matter. The type of patients seen by the Physician would matter too. Insurance only, Pediatric vs Geriatric, type of Surgery performed and so forth might influence results."

"So, many factors can affect an assessment tool. It will be hard, but I guess not impossible, to produce an evaluation of competency for over 20% of the physicians in our country. The problem is how to do it and how accurate will it be, considering all the potential variables there are. As importantly, we should preserve a Physician's own right to have an opinion on when he or she should stop practicing medicine."

"While we are at it, how about we do cognitive

competency tests on other professions to determine if they can keep their certifications or whatever? How about even evaluating older elected government people, like US Senators, for any competency changes with age?"

There was a good amount of clapping around the room as Hank took his seat.

Dr. Moritz spoke next: "Emma, Jack, Hank, thank you for your discussion points. I agree that it will be hard to develop an older physician competency assessment, but I feel like there will be efforts to do so. Regulation and enforcement of assessments will generate a lot of discussion."

***

Dr. Moritz continued: "My second question for the group today is also prompted by Emma's observation on the aging of American Physicians. Given the increasing number of over 65 years old Physicians, there obviously will be significant decreases in the number actually practicing medicine in the coming years. Data are predicting a general shortage of Physicians in the near future. Some estimates say a shortage of over 90,000 by 2020. We also know that, due to our recent Government mandated Health Care plans, it is predicted that at least 20,000-26,000 more specifically trained Primary Care Physicians will be required by 2020. So, let's hear from others here today about some methods or approaches that might help alleviate this anticipated shortfall of Physicians in the next few years."

Jessica, a second year Oncology Resident asked to speak immediately: "I have recently looked at the gender distribution in Medical School graduates and specialty practices. In 2015, females made up 47.5% of the graduates. Importantly, and to a point you just made, more female graduates become Family Practice Physicians, Pediatricians and Obstetricians than male graduates. Family Medicine is certainly a large chunk of Primary Care Physicians. Male graduates have higher percentages entering subspecialties such as Surgery, Emergency, Anesthesiology, and Radiology."

"So, I would offer that one possibly helpful solution would be to enroll and graduate from Medical Schools a higher percent of females. We also know that, presently at least, women have a longer life expectancy than men. So maybe they would be in practice longer."

Moritz responded: "Good points to consider, Jessica. I might challenge you a little bit. Possibly other factors such as child bearing and family responsibilities could affect the age of elective retirement of female Physicians. However, off the top of my head. I do not know the comparisons of elective retirement ages of men and women Physicians. You might look into this consideration closer and include it in your opinion. Maybe you can research some of that data and give us a brief feedback on the question at our meeting next month."

Jessica said she would make a commitment to do this.

Dr. Moritz was looking for further ideas: "How about other discussion. Does anyone have suggestions on how to graduate more Physicians to meet demands through changes in education approaches?"

Marina, a 4th year Medical Student spoke up: "I was thinking that maybe we could shorten Medical School by a few months, maybe even a year. That would, in the long run, get Medical Students out into a Residency sooner. Also, maybe if the duration of a Residency were cut, say, to 2 ½ years instead of 3 years, we would get trained Physicians into medical practice sooner. This would then translate into more Medical School admissions because there would be a new 1st year class every three years, rather than every 4 years. Finally, the shorter Residency would result in trained Physicians entering practice a few months sooner."

Dr. Moritz said: "Anyone have a comment on Marina's idea?"

Pete, who was also in his 4th year of Medical School, raised his hand, got a nod from Dr. Moritz, and then spoke:

"I think that a few of the basic science courses of the first two years of Medical School could be combined to shorten the first 2 years down to 1 ½ years. Increased amounts of teaching using more simulator types could be made available to students. Also, increased internet sites designed by our Faculty using algorithm methods to teach aspects of the clinical rotations could be utilized more effectively. Algorithm approaches are already in use for many clinical disease conditions."

"I also believe that Residents could be called upon for more teaching in the 3rd and 4th clinical years of Medical School. This would not replace the Academic Professors' teaching role, but it could supplement it. An increased emphasis on Resident's more formal teaching would also be valuable for the Residents as they prepare to enter into their own practice. I feel that if you have to teach something, you will know it better yourself. This would be a positive for the Resident and their future patients."

Dr. Moritz spoke next: "Thank you Marina and Pete for your comments. Some of your ideas should be considered it seems to me. I do have a question or hesitation about too much machine learning and the algorithm approach. Will this possibly hurt the student Physician's own thinking process? The Medical Student must learn to decide on and gather appropriate objective data, think about a differential diagnosis, and formulate a correct treatment plan for a specific patient that is actually in front of them. I think students' minds must be challenged and practiced in real life situations to achieve accuracy consistently. If the thinking process is always done for you by a machine, will you be as well prepared to deliver accurate medicine on your own? A balanced approach should probably be utilized."

"I like your suggestion of requiring more specific teaching by Residents. I am not sure how this fits in with resolving the anticipated Physician shortage we are facing. However, I agree that it would help each Physician's communication with patients, peers, and the community in their future practice. Do we have other comments from our group here? We have some time left for more discussion."

Norm, a 2nd year Resident in Oncology was

raising his hand to get Dr. Moritz's attention. Moritz said: "Yes, Norm, go ahead with your comment."

Norm spoke: 'I have ambivalent feelings about this, but how about increasing the number of Primary Care Physicians by increasing the number of 'for profit' Medical Schools and Osteopathic Medical Colleges? Up until recent years, most of the new Medical Schools in the USA have been non-profit Public facilities. We know that several 'for profit' Medical Schools have existed in the Caribbean for several years. A number of their graduates come to America and apply for Internships and Residencies. Now, for the last few years, I believe, there have been a few 'for profit' Medical Schools and Hospitals started in the United States."

Continuing, Norm said: "Many of Osteopathic Medicine graduates choose Residencies and careers in Primary Care. Several also practice in rural or low population communities. So, this approach could help fill some of the gap in our expected increased need for Primary Care Physician subspecialists in the future. I believe also, that their medical practice fees are covered the same as traditional MD. fees by many insurance programs. More 'for profit' traditional

Medical Schools could also be established at the same time."

Dr. Moritz thanked Norm for his comments and then asked for reactions from the group. Some concerns brought up were the financial viability and assurance of funding sources supporting any new 'for profit' Schools. Maybe more State funding would draw those Schools to locate in a particular State. Possibly with vested interests in the location of Schools, enhanced pursuit and availability of Federal student loans would occur, depending on the amount of the State's influence in Washington, D.C. The donations from local private estates or businesses were other suggestions brought up as possible sources of funding.

Dr. Moritz expressed the opinion that an increase in 'for profit' Medical School graduates might overwhelm the availability of existing accredited Residency positions. He also was concerned about how to insure and measure that the appropriate standards of educational content, and one on one patient contact training, would be met by all new 'for profit' schools.

Moritz also noted that an additional approach could be to increase the number of Physician Assistant training programs. This would help reduce some of the work load on Physicians. Advanced degree Nurses could also be utilized more frequently.

At 2:00 PM, Moritz thanked everyone for coming to this discussion of some current issues relative to their profession. He wished everyone good luck as they left for their work. Several of those attending the meeting thanked and complimented him for taking time to commit to these sessions.

After the room emptied, Dr. Moritz walked back to the office in his laboratory. He needed to review once again some points he wanted to make at the pending Committee meeting tomorrow morning.

11

Victor Moritz was up early on this day of the second Committee meeting. Breakfast, kennel Shadow, feed steers, and then a shower. When ready to leave the cabin, he picked up his Trail Camera from a shelf in the pantry room, checked its battery, and put it in his briefcase.   Outside was another nice autumn morning.

Moritz arrived at the laboratory before anyone else of his group. He went through his power point figures of some recent confirmatory data he might present at this second Committee meeting.

His presentation today would also include notifying the Committee of recent grant money committed to him from an organization named 'The Independent Cancer Cure Pharmaceutical Foundation' (ICCPF).   The Foundation's grant to Moritz will provide a small portion of his personal salary. More importantly, the award supports both his basic research and his clinical study if and when it is approved. The award promised funding for a total of 5 years.

This new award was not limited to supporting Moritz's studies on prostate cancer metastases to bone. It was awarded in part to fund a new observation by his lab. This recent information had not yet been published or discussed with anyone outside of his research group, except for the inclusion of the findings in his application to ICCPF.

These new observations were far from being fully investigated as yet. However, if Moritz's approach to treating metastatic prostate cancer in bone proved helpful and curative, his method might also be used in breast cancer bone metastases. Moritz's latest research data was very interesting to the ICCPF, since 70-80% of women with advanced metastatic breast cancer develop bone metastases. This is similar to the high rate of prostate cancer metastases to bone.

At 8:30 AM Moritz came out of his lab office and greeted his research group. All three had arrived and were preparing experiments for the day. He said: "Wish me luck, team." They all did, and he then left the lab and walked to the conference room to meet with the Committee.

Moritz was the first to arrive for the meeting which was to start at 9:00 AM. He began setting up the visual aid equipment in case he had the opportunity to use it today. Dr. Phil Johnson was next to arrive, greeted Moritz, took a seat and began reviewing some paperwork he had with him. In a couple of minutes, Dr. Lopez entered. She smiled a greeting to Moritz and Johnson, then found a seat across from them. Rob Olson arrived next, said 'Hello" to the others and sat down.

At 9:10 AM, Dr. Jerry Smith and Dr. David Green, with Michael Jones, the Associate Chairman of the Lake View financial office, arrived for the meeting. Mr. Jones was introduced to and shook hands with Rob Olson. Already knowing all the Faculty in the room, he acknowledged each by name and then took a seat beside Dr. David Green, chairman of the Committee. Green and Jones spoke to each other in hushed tones for a minute or so.

***

Dr. Green opened the meeting: "Dr. Moritz, there are a few issues that remain for further discussion. Let's start with an issue related to Dr. Lopez's query at our last meeting. The crux of the question was weighing the patient benefits against the costs, financial and personal, when entering terminally ill patients into a clinical study. Maybe one should consider continuing them in Palliative or Hospice care at such a late stage of their illness."

Moritz got up from his chair to respond: "Since you used the terms Palliative and Hospice care, I will speak to this first. These terms sometimes are not totally understood by patients or clearly defined by those outlining the difference in the options. So, let me define what I understand about these terms."

"Yes, our study will only enroll patients classified as terminal. Their disease is going to kill them within months. Their disease has progressed despite all known treatments tried. These patients can consciously decide not to try any more treatments. Such patients with a terminal condition from prostate cancer metastases can elect Hospice or Palliative care."

"Those selecting Hospice care usually have a life expectancy of less than a year. The goal of their care is relieving symptoms, by using appropriate comforting care and medications, which commonly includes pain and sedative approaches, along with emotional support of the patient and their family. Hospice patients are not candidates for our study since they are not seeking any more specific possible curative treatment for their disease."

"Patients in Palliative care can also be terminal, but they might not always be terminal. Patients in Palliative care programs, in addition to receiving care for symptoms and supportive measures, often select to have potentially curative cares continued. Also, they might want new possibly curative measures initiated."

"The study I am proposing, therefore, would not

enter patients who have chosen Hospice care. Patients with terminal illness from prostate cancer bone metastases that we will approach for study enrollment may be receiving cares at various levels in the Hospital, maybe in Palliative care programs or receiving care at home."

Moritz continued: "Regarding costs of the study, there are several things I will clarify, especially since Michael is here. Bottom line, my already awarded and pending grant money will pay for any study related costs. If a patient is already hospitalized at Lake View, our grant money pays costs due to the study that are above the regular charges to the patient. Let me remind you, this will not happen very often. Rarely will a study patient be admitted to the Hospital for the study. Most study patients will be treated and evaluated in the outpatient clinic facility. The clinic will be reimbursed for the extra expenses incurredby the study."

"Extra laboratory analyses, imaging, supplies used for the study and so on will be paid for by our grant money. Thus, no additional costs to the hospital will be left uncovered due to the study patients. The grant money also will be funding two Research Nurses' salaries. These Research Nurses will perform any extra procedures required by the study, such as the intravenous administration of the Nanosphere Complex. They will alternate 'on call' responsibilities for any care or question that is relative to the study, beyond the regular care the patient already required before they entered the study."

"Now, what if a patient is enrolled in the study, but at the time is not in the Lake View area nor a patient of a Lake View Physician? The study grants will pay for those patient's transfer to Lake View and subsequent Hospital clinic costs, or overnight charges if necessary. Hence, I do not see any extra costs this Hospital will have to cover as a result of these patients. As a matter of fact, I might even see some benefits to Lake View. Maybe the efforts of the study will be recognized by a couple of charitable persons that feel like rewarding Lake View through a new private financial donation. Of course, I realize there are also risks. If iatrogenic events or other mishaps occur during the study, it would certainly be a negative for the Hospital, as well as for our research."

At this point, Dr. Moritz paused and took a drink from his glass of water. After a few moments, he faced the group again, and continued to speak: "Another aspect of this discussion is something you, Dr. Green, alluded to at our last meeting. You noted that metastatic prostate cancer occurs most frequently in older men. You suggested maybe there should not be such a time consuming and expensive effort exerted for these patients. The fact that many prostate cancer metastases to bone occurs in elderly men is true. That brings up a philosophical issue to me. I sense what I consider an undesirable trend in medical care these days. In my mind, it coincides with the increase in Federal Government's involvement in regulation and funding of Health Care."

"The trend, at least in my maybe suspicious reasoning, is to start treating elderly patients as dying patients sooner than might be appropriate. Let me explore with you what I am feeling. Are Physicians starting to lengthen out the time between certain studies as their patients grow older? If there is a trend towards this, is it done based on scientific clinical data and observations, or something else, like reimbursement costs? Let's say, are colonoscopies scheduled less frequently after a certain age, instead of the frequency when younger? If so, are there sound reasons for that? Are cardiac ECHO's or arterial ultrasound evaluations done less frequently as the patient ages? These are just random examples I picked, but I feel such trends may be occurring with various medical cares and procedures. This might especially be a relevant question in elderly patients with cancer."

"Are care guidelines being altered by the expectation that a known cancer will kill the patient before the colon, heart, or other problems will? In the short term, health care dollars might be saved by fewer studies on the elderly cancer patient. However, just around the corner might be a successful cancer treatment for this patient. So, let's say that the cancer is now successfully treated and cured."

"However, what if this elderly cancer patient's colon, heart or other disease process was not followed as regularly or aggressively as when he or she was younger and cancer free? Now, these diseases kill the cancer cured patient sooner than if that elderly cancer patient had been followed closely and treated for their other issues when those other diseases were actually treatable. Maybe their other medical problems would have been picked up by more frequent and usual screening procedures, rather than being deleted or spread out longer merely because the cancer patient was elderly. Thus, the cancer cured patient dies earlier than necessary."

Moritz continued: "So, to repeat my scenario,

let's admit the Health Care costs were less because of fewer studies in that elderly patient who had cancer. Although the cancer was then cured by a newly discovered treatment, death was still earlier than necessary because other possible medical causes of death had not been followed closely and treated vigorously in the elderly cancer patient."

"Alternatively, with frequent cares and treatments of the other disease processes, coupled with curing the cancer, a longer elderly life might have been possible. Now, certainly the cost would be more Health Care dollars. I wonder what our politicians in Government are choosing now when they insert themselves into medical practice decisions? I hope I am wrong in my thinking about this as a trend in elderly medicine, but I worry on it. Are there other medical care providers concerned about this, or is it not an issue?"

"I have found some support for my opinion. Recently the International Society of Geriatric Oncology has suggested a new guideline. The recommendation was that 'Physicians should decide on prostate cancer treatment in the elderly according to the individual's fitness and health status, and not just their age'."

"I know, I need more information and hard data to support my feeling of the 'Trend'. So, I apologize, Dr. Green and others here, for this digression. Let me get back on topic. Are there more questions about my study that you need further information on?"

***

Rob Olson, the lay person on the Committee, indicated he wanted to speak: "Dr. Moritz, I think the question you just talked about is certainly thought provoking, relevant, and deserves more consideration at many levels."

"However, I do believe you have digressed quite a bit from the assignment for this Committee. So, I would like to get back to your clinical study. Dr. Moritz, could you review for me, in relatively general terms, the Phases of Clinical Trials, and indicate where your study fits in with the National Cancer Institute's (NCI) Clinical Trials Phases. I am sure others on the Committee are familiar with this, but I would like a brief review."

Moritz responded: "Mr. Olson, thanks for the question. My first point is that one objective of a NCI Phase 1 Clinical Trial is to decide how the new treatment can be given. For our study, which uses Nanospheres with an attached Antibody, intravenous injection is the only choice. We cannot use the digestive tract or an intramuscular injection. So that is already settled."

"Second point. We have approval from the NCI to combine parts of Phase 1 and Phase 2 in our Trial. The Phase 1 part of our trial will determine a safe dose of the Nanosphere Complex. This will be done by enrolling patients into 3 different dose groups of 15 patients each."

"Our starting point dose has been decided upon by our in vivo primate study's data, then adjusted for weight of our patients. So, 15 patients will receive Dose 1. Another 15 patients will receive 3 times the concentration of Dose 1, and another 15 patients will receive 5 times the concentration of Dose 1. Each patient will receive one intravenous infusion of their designated dose every 3 weeks for 3 doses. The variable is the different concentrations of the Nanosphere Complex. Patients will be randomly enrolled into one or the other of the doses upon their entry into the study. Side effects, if any, whether clinical or laboratory, will be monitored as we treat patients."

"This Phase 1 evaluation will simultaneously involve aspects of a typical Phase 2 objective. One question related to Phase 2 that will be considered and answered is an evaluation of whether or not the treatment has some benefit. To study this, we will evaluate if the size, growth, or invasive progress of the metastatic bone cancer is altered in any of the treated patients. Did the treatment with any of the three doses have an effect on the prostate's cancer cell metastases? If so, which dose was beneficial? Did the higher dose cause side effects or was it most beneficial? Evaluations of organ function and blood markers will also be recorded. These results will be compared to baseline values that were obtained when the patient enters the study"

"In addition to those things I have just mentioned, we have a supplementary goal as part of the Phase 2 aspect. We will try to learn if other organ systems of the patient's body are changing after receiving the Nanosphere Complex. That is, did some of the Nanosphere Complex lodge in non-metastatic sites and affect that organ's function? This could be a negative finding in our study. We found no evidence of this in any animal studies. Still, we will look for this during our clinical study."

"There is a NCI Phase 3 Clinical Trial program. The main focus in Phase 3 is to determine if the new treatment being studied works better than the standard therapies already being used. These Phase 3 studies require the enrollment of hundreds of patients for satisfactory statistical analysis of the data. Our study here at Lake View is not nearly close to a Phase 3 trial at this time. Such a Phase would require an enrollment study conducted at several cancer facilities to obtain a sufficient number of patients to be statistically valid."

After speaking, Dr. Moritz sat back down to take another brief break. He then asked: "Mr. Olson, did I clarify this issue to your satisfaction?"

Rob Olson said: "You certainly did and thank you for that."

Dr. David Green asked if anyone else had a question today. Dr. Jerry Smith raised his hand. Green nodded to go ahead.

Smith said: "I actually had a question earlier about the dose. You answered it, I guess, by including the 3 different dose groups you plan. I think basing the human dose on animal, even primate, experimental data might not be the most accurate way to start, but that seems to be the best option you have."

Moritz responded: "When we submitted our plan to the NIH/NCI review board, they agreed our approach was a reasonable starting point. If there is an obvious problem with any dose after the first few patients, the NIH/NCI review board will be notified. We will then discuss with them altering our protocol if necessary. We would also certainly report any problem to this Committee."

Dr. Phil Johnson asked to speak, and after a nod from David Green, said: "Victor, it seems to me that if some of your patients have metastatic sites other than bone, the Nanosphere Complex might target them as well. That might be a good thing! What is you comment on this possibility?"

Victor responded: "Phil, we plan to enter patients with PET scan confirmation of bone cancer metastases only. Your question is one we have also thought about. We are doing preliminary studies in the lab now to see if the Nanosphere Complex will target other tissues that have metastatic prostate cancer cell involvement and are possibly producing Antigen X on their surface. These are very preliminary experiments and we have no data to report yet. We are uncertain if the metastatic prostate cells in other organs have Antigen X."

There was another several minutes talking over minor points, essentially on the data Dr. Moritz had presented at the first meeting. After these discussions had closed, Dr. David Green said he would like for Michael Jones of the financial office to have a few minutes with the Committee.

***

The financial office representative had come prepared with a one page handout that he passed around to each member of the Committee. Michael Jones was a youthful age 32 athletic looking man. He was dressed in a nicely fitted suit with his shirt open at the collar. Single and handsome. He was obviously up to speed technologically with both his I-phone and lightweight laptop accompanying him to the meeting, and likely with him almost always wherever he went.

Mike began speaking: "Well, Dr. Green, thank you for inviting me here today. As probably all of the faculty at his meeting already know, the Lake View organization has a newly formed Committee called the 'Faculty Equity Committee'. David and I are Co-founders of this new Committee which now has 8 members, 4 from Administration and 4 from the Faculty. Follow the handout I gave you, it outlines the points I want to cover. We are meeting with all Lake View Faculty that have pending or already awarded research grants. The meeting here with Dr. Moritz's review Committee was timely for our office."

Jones continued: "One interest of the new Faculty Equity Committee is to supplement the financial support of certain unequally paid Faculty. One example are those who have not yet been successful in obtaining research funding on their own. Others are faculty who have recently lost grant funds during competitive renewal attempts. Thus, their salary has suffered since grants usually include some of a faculty's salary, and Lake View struggles to make up the difference.

We are working with the Lake View Administration to pass several new financial decisions to insure more Faculty salary equality at our Center. One effort underway is lobbying Federal Granting Agencies like NIH, to convince them to increase the percent of 'Indirect Costs' they presently pay on Awarded grants. As you know, Institutions that receive grants use the item designated 'Indirect Cost' dollars to pay some costs of the Institution. This includes, for example, administering the grant award, and supplying the offices and laboratory facilities used in the research, and other relevant overhead costs."

"The requested increase in 'Indirect Costs' would go to a special fund of our new Faculty Equity Committee. This money will then be distributed to our non-funded Research Faculty to improve their salary. Some of the extra overhead money will also be used to give seed money to unfunded Faculty for their, as yet unfunded, research ideas. This question with Federal Granting Agencies is under negotiation discussions at this time."

"Now, I refer you to the second point that is outlined in your handout, near the middle of the page. We know that many non-government private programs and charitable donated financial grants usually do not have a specific line item for 'Indirect Costs'. Neither do some other sources of funds like certain Pharmaceutical Companies that grant research funds to our Faculty. While some 'Indirect Costs' are usually obtained from these types of awards, it is variable and uncertain as to what amount will be available for Lake View's Administration to use."

"Therefore, starting this week, and from now on, these types of grant awards to our Faculty will be assessed 10% of the amount of the award. Approximately half of that will go to Lake View to cover the 'Indirect Costs' for handling the grant. The other 5% will go to and be distributed by the Faculty Equity Committee as I have just described."

"These are two examples of pursuing Faculty equity that will result from our newly developed Committee. We hope to encourage other institutions like us to consider adopting plans such as ours."

By this time, Victor Moritz, Phil Johnson, and Rebecca Lopez were looking at each other, hardly believing what they had just heard. Jerry Smith, presently with no extramural research funding, was looking down, giving the appearance of studying the handout that Mike Jones had circulated. David Green was looking at Mike, nodding with obvious support of the concept and presentation.

Mike Jones, after a pause, said: "So that is essentially the message I wanted to deliver today. I will be presenting this to all the Departments of Lake View during the next 3 weeks. Please feel free to give me some feedback if you want. I know that Dr. Moritz will be affected soon. Our office has just been notified of his recent research award from the ICCPF. Probably no one here except Dr. Moritz has heard about this recent good news for his research program."

Victor Moritz asked Dr. Green if he could say a few words in response, and he was given the opportunity.

***

Victor got up from his chair and began: "Mike, I do have a few points and some opinions to offer at this time. One point for us to note is that my contract with Lake View states that my efforts are 25 % research, 25% teaching, and 50% clinical care. I believe that this is generally the contract of all

Clinical-Science Faculty at Lake View."

"Now consider this. If I have funded research grants, they will pay up to 25% of my salary. That saves Lake View 25% of my salary for the duration of the grants. Lake View pays only the other 75% of my salary. This 75% salary portion is payment for my teaching and clinical patient care. I point out to you, Mike, that 75% of salary paid to me by Lake View is not anywhere near the revenue generated by my clinical care of Oncology patients. All my Physician fees go to Lake View, not me. Lake View laboratory fees, in Hospital room fees, imaging costs for the patient, and so on, all go to Lake View. My salary is a relatively small percent of all these generated incomes that the Lake View Hospital and services receives from my care of patients"

"Next, let's say the Federal Grant Agencies agree to your request to use a higher percent of the grant money for 'Indirect Costs'. How will that happen? It is unlikely that these government agencies will give my awarded grant extra money. Lake View will take the additional amount directly from my grant's already funded amount. That means less money in the grant for my laboratory's research expenses. The same will happen by the assessment of 10% from other funding sources."

"Now you plan not only to take more of my research generated money, but you will distribute it to other members of the Faculty".

"Specifically, you said it is going to Faculty that are unfunded for their own research. These are dollars that I competed for by doing the research and the grant application process. These are dollars that could have helped my team's research progress."

"In my opinion, such an approach will inevitably lead to increasing numbers of Lake View Faculty making less effort to obtain their own research grants. This 'Faculty Equity Pay' will bring about lethargy and poor effort in a certain percent of your Faculty. Why should they work extra time in the laboratory and spend many hours writing grants? They will be given money from someone else's funded grants to help bring them to a higher (equality) pay scale?"

"This smells to me like the beginning of Socialism practices here at Lake View."

"I strongly disagree with this. Each of our Faculty should use their reason, individual effort and original thoughts to continue to try to obtain research funding to support a portion of their salary, if that is what they were hired, in part, to do. Lake View's own revenues should continue to pay all their salary until they obtain grant support for the research portion of it. If their earnest research efforts are not rewarded with outside funding, those Faculty members should be allowed to withdraw from the research portion of their job description contract. Then they can spend all of their time on Clinical Care and Teaching. Lake View would then pay them appropriate 100% amounts from their patient generated income. Don't penalize Faculty who have successfully obtained research funding by the methods you have described this morning."

"So, what else will happen if this plan of your new 'Faculty Equity Committee' is followed? I believe Lake View's prestige as an excellent Medical Research and science based Medical Center will decline. This will happen in part because of the withdrawal of many non-funded Faculty from the ranks of science based competitive Physicians. Coupled with that, Lake View will also lose some of the successfully funded research Faculty. They will leave your program because you are scalping them for their success."

"I sincerely hope the Government agencies, such as the NIH and the National Cancer Institute, do not agree with your requests to use more of their granted research money for your scheme."

Amazingly, to Moritz's surprise, Phil, Rob, and

Rebecca individually spoke out with: "Yes," "Hear, Hear," and "Strongly Agree." Mike Jones looked at Dr. David Green for some support. Dr. Green remained quiet at this time.

Shortly after this, looking directly at Victor Moritz, Mike said: "Dr. Moritz, I expected that you would have a different opinion on this issue. However, our Faculty Equity Committee will continue to work to implement their plans. We believe many of our ideas will be accepted. After all, Dr. Moritz, we think that you have an obligation of service and sacrifice to others, and not just to exist and be productive only for your own sake."

Mike looked around the table and saw only Smith and Green agreeing with him.

Dr. Victor Moritz shook his head back and forth, signaling disbelief, then sat down and had another drink of water. He then said: "Are you going to come after a share of my rural home site next?"

***

After a minute or so of silence, Dr. David Green spoke: "Dr. Moritz, I would appreciate your giving the Committee a brief summary of this recently awarded grant from the ICCPF."

Moritz stood, not thanking Green for the opportunity, and then spoke: "This recent award from the ICCPF was awarded primarily to help support our Nanosphere Complex research and treatment of metastatic prostate cancer to bone, the study we have been discussing at these Committee meetings. We applied for the grant over a year ago. The application gave background experimental details and outlined our planned clinical study."

"Importantly as well, this grant application also included our preliminary data of other experiments. This new data has never been presented yet to the public. However, an Abstract outlining the initial findings has been accepted for presentation at the next American Society of Clinical Oncology meeting. I now share with you some of the essentials of our new finding, hoping you keep this held confidential until the Award is announced and our Abstract is published at the National level."

"As many of you know, a major site of metastases by both prostate and breast cancer is bone, especially hip, spine and pelvis. There is much research trying to clarify the reasons for this. The general thinking and much research is focused on some principal areas. First, there are interactions between the cancer cells of breast and prostate with factors of bone's microenvironment.

Some cells from the original tumor often are changed as they progress and deposit in bone niches, which are small cavities present in the interlining of bone. Apparently, some unique characteristic of bone has led to the favorable nesting environment for these rogue prostate and breast cancer cells. Then, these metastatic cancer cells start a large tumor growth or become destructive to the bone through lysis and breakdown mechanisms."

"This leads me to a few words about our new project. We have discovered that breast cancer cells that have metastasized to bone have an Antigen on their surface that is very similar to Antigen X that we have found on prostate cancer cells in bone metastases. We are calling this Antigen X-2. In fact, we find that Antibody Y, which attaches to Antigen X on metastatic prostate cancer cells, also attaches just as firmly to Antigen X-2 on metastatic breast cancer cells in bone."

"This new finding has led the ICCPF to promise an additional financial supplement to the recent grant award to our laboratory. Mike, this information is being released to your financial office by the ICCPF next week. With that additional grant money, we will start experimental animal studies similar to those we did recently with bone metastatic prostate cancer. We will determine if our Nanosphere Complex can attack these metastatic breast cancer cells in bone, just as with metastatic prostate cancer cells in bone."

"We started this research last year. As I indicated before, we know that nearly 7 out of 10 late breast cancer patients suffer from bone metastases. This is about the same rate as prostate cancer metastases to bone. We thought there might be something similar in each event. If so, maybe there is a treatment, like our Nanosphere Complex, that will help cure each. We hope to have found a clue to start with."

Dr. Moritz paused briefly, and then continued speaking, while looking directly at David Green and Jerry Smith: "Now, I know you, David and Jerry, are working on breast cancer as your research interest. So, you might think I am encroaching on your territory. However, the emphasis of your work is on the origin and factors that trigger the beginning of breast cancer. Your research is a very important question to solve. I see no conflict here with your research goals. Our research effort is on bone metastases and a possible cure for that problem, whether the origin is from prostate or breast. That is our emphasis."

Dr. David Green and Dr. Jerry Smith remained

quiet. However, Dr. Phil Johnson raised his hand and proceeded to speak: "Victor, what is your working hypothesis here for how these two different metastatic cancer cells have produced a similar new surface Antigen, X and X-2? Is it present before or after metastasis to the bone?"

Dr. Moritz responded: "Phil, thanks for your question. We do not find Antigen X or Antigen X -2 on the cancer cells in their original organ site, prostate or breast. Our working hypothesis so far is this. After the cancer cell invasion of bone, the bone site responds to the cancer cell. We feel some factor from the bone's vascular lining, or a bone cell is responsible for the new surface Antigen X and X-2. Maybe some factor secreted from the endothelial cell, which lines the vascular niche, is acting on the invasive cancer cell. Alternatively, maybe there is direct contact between bone and cancer cells which alters the cancer cell's surface to form Antigen X and Antigen X-2."

"Our search for the mechanism that changes a site on the metastasized cancer cell is a high priority for us now. Who knows, maybe if our Nanosphere Complex can target and kill bone metastatic prostate cancer cells, it might work also on metastatic breast cancer cells in bone. There is a lot of work ahead to clarify these questions."

"So, we are thankful for and excited about this new finding. Dr. Chen has even drawn several 'red stars' on the special lab notebook we use for this project's research findings and progress."

Victor Moritz sat down. As he did so, he noted Jerry Smith and David Green having some special eye contact and facial expressions between themselves. This was also obviously noted by other members of the Committee.

Dr. David Green said: "It is past lunch time. I think any final questions for Dr. Moritz and our Committee's vote will have to wait until another meeting, later this week or early next. My office will contact each of you. For now, we are adjourned."

***

As the group left the room, there were two separate gatherings talking among themselves. Rob Olson, Phil Johnson, and Rebeca Lopez, complimenting Victor on his grant awards, were talking together. The other three, David Green, Jerry Smith and Mike Jones, stopped in the hallway, were also seemingly talking about the breast cancer metastases observations of Dr. Moritz. Both groups finally dispersed after several minutes.

Victor Moritz stopped by the Hospital deli for a

sandwich and apple. He then went out to a table in the lawn where he and Ruth had been just two days ago. He thought of their good times this past week-end, ate lunch, and then headed to the laboratory. He suspected David Green and Jerry Smith were up to something. He was thinking of a plan of his own.

12

After lunch break, Dr. Victor Moritz realized it was too late to go to the lab before making daily rounds to see his patients on the Oncology ward. He decided he would stop by the lab to talk with Dr. Chen later in the afternoon.

At two o'clock, Moritz started visiting his patients, accompanied by the 2 Residents working on this Oncology ward and the Head Nurse. The Medical Students assigned to the ward were at a Pathology Conference at this time today. Therefore, rounds were a little more efficient. The Residents presented the patients, the results of their recent laboratory or imaging studies, and a summary of their medical progress the last 24 hours. As usual, Dr. Moritz spoke with each patient and performed a brief physical exam as warranted, depending on the patient's problem.

One patient had a new medical issue that had occurred over the last 24 hours. The 60 year old male, who previously had prostate cancer, was now in his 4th week of chemotherapy for Stage 2 lymphoma. A complication of his chemotherapy had occurred. A blood clot formed in the main vein of his left leg. Ultrasound showed the clot to extend from just below his groin to the knee. There was swelling and some discoloration of the leg. A significant concern was that a piece of the clot, called an embolus, might break off the main clot and float through the venous system to the lungs or other vital organs. This could compromise organ function, sometimes even causing death.

Therefore, this patient was now being treated with a medicine that was stopping further enlarging of the clot formation and would help prevent the other potential complications caused by an embolus. This anticoagulating medicine would have to be used by the patient for several weeks or months, even after completion of the chemotherapy. Elastic pressure stockings, elevation and mobilization of the leg were also being carried out. Dr. Moritz tried to be reassuring to the patient that the clot will eventually resolve. However, he was realistic about the need for the anticoagulation medication and warned about additional potential problems if the present clot in the leg was not treated correctly.

Patient rounds took only one and a half hours. After a final discussion with the Residents and Head Nurse, Moritz wrote a short electronic note on each patient, left the ward and went to his office in the clinic.

He had no patients scheduled for clinic today, but there were a couple messages from the Staff regarding outpatient questions they had received and responded to. The Staff's responses to these questions were to Moritz's satisfaction, so he personally did not return calls to those patients at this time. These patients were, in any event, already scheduled for clinic visits in the latter part of this week.

Another message was especially concerning. It had been sent to his Clinic e-main address early this morning. The message read: "Otto Zellers was admitted to the cardiac Intensive Care Unit Sunday night at 8:30 PM. Zellers had experienced a transient fainting episode and fell while at home. Although extremely weak, after regaining consciousness he was able to call 911. He was then transported to Lake View Hospital by local EMS. Cardiac stabilization and evaluation continued through the night and Monday. He is stable at this time, being treated with anti-arrhythmic medications. He is scheduled to receive an indwelling Pacemaker/Defibrillator early tomorrow morning. He asked that you be notified of these recent events."

Victor had a sudden bolt of fright, and sincere concern for his good friend. He immediately called the cardiac ward. He asked if Dr. Zellers was still stable and if he could receive brief visitors this evening.

The Nurse in charge said: "Yes, Dr. Zellers is stable and resting. He has asked if we have heard from you, Dr. Moritz. You would be allowed 15 minutes to visit if you came in before 9:00 PM this evening."

Moritz thanked the Nurse and hung up the phone somewhat relieved, but worried. He then left the clinic office and went directly to his laboratory to speak with Dr. Chen.

* * *

Li Chen was alone still working in the lab this late in the afternoon. Mark and Charlie had finished their experiments earlier and had gone to the Science Building's auditorium to hear a lecture by a visiting Oncologist from the University of Michigan. They both had planned on going to their homes after the lecture.

Chen and Moritz greeted each other as he entered the laboratory. Dr. Chen had just finished making an entry into the Red Star Notebook. This notebook, as Moritz noted earlier today at the Committee meeting, contains the data on the just discovered metastatic breast cancer cell Antigen X-2. She closed the notebook and placed it on the lab bench that she had been working at.

Moritz said: "Li, how have you been today? Talk to me some about your day and then I will catch you up on the latest Committee meeting."

Dr. Chen gave Moritz a brief informative summary of today's work. She had confirmed tight binding of Antibody Y to Antigen X-2, the antigen present on breast cancer cells that had metastasized to bone, in the experimental animal studies. Mark and Charlie had seen the results of Dr. Chen's good progress today before they left for the lecture. Mark had even asked Dr. Chen if he could look at the data she had entered in the Red Star Notebook! She had shown him the recent data entry and discussed with him some future experiments that possibly he could conduct that would help with this breast cancer metastasis project. He had left the lab heading for the lecture in good spirits.

Li did not tell Moritz what experiments she had told Mark about, and smiling as she spoke, let him hang on a string about what those experiments might be. Moritz took this good naturedly.

Then also smiling, he said: "Li, just let me know when these additional experimental results are ready to discuss. I trust your good judgement."

Moritz gave Li a review of today's Committee meeting. She was surprised at the financial office's plan to take more of the Faculty's grant dollars for administrative costs and the Faculty Equity Committee's plan. Dr. Chen asked Moritz if this action could lead to a compromise in her salary. Since the majority of her salary is funded through awarded grant money, could this action affect her job and income? Moritz told Li that her salary support was one of the most important items in all of his grant applications. He assured her of his absolute and total commitment to protect the level of her salary and her deserved merit raises.

Moritz continued and told her he tried to present some valid objections to the new plan from Lake View's financial group. However, he admitted that it seemed like their plan was to go full steam ahead. Victor told Li of the support he had received from Olson, Johnson, and Lopez when he presented his views on the issue. He also mentioned his feelings that Dr. Green and Jerry Smith were pretty quiet, but likely angry about this new work by Li and himself on breast cancer metastases to bone.

As he finished talking of the meeting, Moritz said: "Li, we have the fact that Green and Smith have visited you in the lab, pressured, threatened and berated you. I am hoping they will not try that again. If they do, stand your ground, do not talk with them. Give me a call or Text immediately. I will try to get here in time to confront them."

Victor sensed an increased tension in Dr. Chen. He reached out, took hold of her trembling hand and said: "Hang in there Li, I will be bringing this nasty business up at the next Committee meeting and also with the Director of Science here at Lake View. We will at least ask for some disciplinary action. It is important that we report their behavior. Who knows, maybe intimidation of other research persons has happened here at Lake View before or recently."

Moritz then suggested to Dr. Chen that she should go home a little early today and take it easy on herself. She thanked him, then put away some lab materials and shut off those instruments that required a manual shutdown. After taking off her lab coat, Li got her purse, put on her jacket and backpack and was ready to leave. She asked: "Dr. Moritz, do you want to look at the results in the Red Star Notebook anymore today?"

Moritz said: "Yes, Li, just leave it out there on the lab bench. I'll look at it some more before I leave. Actually, after I leave the lab, I will be going to see Otto Zellers for a few minutes. Otto was admitted to Lake View Hospital Sunday night because of a cardiac event, and had several procedures since then. They will let me in to visit with him for a few minutes yet tonight."

Li said: "Oh, I am sorry to hear Dr. Zellers is ill. When you go visit, please tell him I wish that he will get better soon."

"I appreciate the update on the Committee Meeting. I'll be in early tomorrow morning. Goodnight Dr. Moritz."

Moritz responded: "I'll give Otto your message, and Li, thanks again for all your hard work every day here in the lab on our projects. Have a good evening."

***

Alone in the laboratory now, Victor took up the Red Star Notebook containing the experiments on the breast cancer metastases project. He found the entries he had not yet seen from last Friday, and read those and the most recent data from today. Everything seemed to have been documented properly. He closed the notebook, smiled as he looked at the large Red Stars on its front, and placed it back on the benchtop that had been otherwise cleared of chemicals, glassware and other paperwork.

Moritz then retrieved from his briefcase the Trail Camera he had brought from home this morning.

He had a suspicious feeling that David Green and Jerry Smith were very angry or jealous about his lab doing experiments and making progress with breast cancer bone metastases. Moritz clearly thought that his latest research was in no way competitive or undercutting their research. However, he felt they acted with restrained but obvious anger during and after the meeting today. He already had experienced their previous intrusion into his lab and their intimidating of Dr. Li Chen. Thus, Moritz had begun to think about the possibility of someone from Green or Smith's group might cross the line again.

With this concern in mind, Moritz had brought the Trail Camera to use and possibly obtain evidence of any intrusion into his lab. He made sure that the Red Star Notebook was in plain sight on the first workbench after entering the door.

Next, he thought over the possible settings of the camera and where he might place it. This camera could capture motion triggered events using an invisible infrared flash with a forward range of 50 feet. He set the wide angle mode of 16 x 8 feet. The camera had an 86 GB DS card and would record the date and time, and then compile the images into a video.

Moritz had checked the batteries in the camera

just this morning and he knew it was working. After making the settings, he placed the camera on an elevated shelf at the end of the lab bench that contained the Red Star Notebook. The camera's position was among some other equipment and not readily obvious. The photo angle included the entrance doorway to Moritz's lab, the lab bench where the Red Star Notebook was, as well as the walking space along this bench.

His conversation with Li had assured him that Mark, Charlie and herself were each going to their homes for the evening and would not be returning to the lab until morning. Moritz turned on the camera. He then gathered his paperwork and briefcase from his office, left the lab and locked the door behind him. The overhead motion sensitive lights went out automatically as he left.

***

Moritz arrived on the Cardiac Unit to speak with Otto Zellers just after the old gentleman Physician, now a patient, had finished his liquid diet evening meal. Otto was giving the Nurse a hard time about the liquids only meal, but she was standing her ground. The Nurse was telling Otto that he was having a soft diet ice cream snack later tonight. However, after midnight, he could only have sips of water because of having the pacemaker/defibrillator placement procedure early in the morning. After that, his dietary restrictions would gradually be lifted.

Moritz had been cleared by the Unit's admission desk to visit Otto for no more than 15-20 minutes. Arriving at Otto's room, he waited until the meal discussion with the Nurse was over before he knocked on the partially open door. He introduced himself to the Nurse.   She said they were expecting him, that she was glad to meet Dr. Moritz, and invited him to come into the room. She checked the readings of Otto's vital signs, oxygen and electrocardiogram monitors and was satisfied. She said to let her know if they needed her for anything, and left the room.

Otto was confined to the bed by an intravenous cannula in his left arm that was administering heart rhythm and other medication from syringes on pumps that were infusing fluids to him from a plastic bag hanging on a pole at his bedside.   He also had an intravenous cannula in his right jugular vein in the neck. This access provided a reading of his venous blood pressure. The arterial blood pressure was being taken non-invasively by a pressure sensor strapped over the artery in his wrist.

Otto smiled as best he could when he saw Victor. Victor went over beside the bed and touched Otto's shoulder and gave it a firm friendly squeeze.

They exchanged greetings and then Victor said: "Otto, I am sorry to see you down, but I am glad you made it to the Hospital. It seems like you have received the appropriate care and treatments. Do you feel like giving me a brief review of what is going on? I won't stay but a few minutes and am happy they allowed me to see you for a while."

Otto spoke after clearing his throat and asking Victor to help him take a sip of water from the glass on his bedside stand: "Victor, I am glad to see you, thanks for coming. It happened Sunday evening a couple hours or so after you and Ruth left my home. I was in the kitchen and felt weak and almost fainted. I made it to a chair at the desk and tried to take my pulse. My pulse was weak. I could rarely detect a distinct heartbeat. In the meantime, I became weaker. I reached for the phone, dialed 911, said 'this is a cardiac emergency,' gave my address and then apparently collapsed."

"Fortunately, I had not yet locked the house door after you and Ruth left. The next thing I was aware of was lying on the kitchen floor and 3 EMS persons working on me. One was starting an intravenous infusion line, another was attaching a blood pressure cuff and securing wires for an electrocardiogram, the 3rd was putting oxygen tubing at my nose."

"I faded in and out of consciousness but felt movement onto a cart, rolling, and being loaded into the EMS van. Then one of the EMS responders was talking on the phone to the ER Physician at the Hospital, and one was driving us with the siren and lights. The 3rd was checking the electrocardiogram, pulse and blood pressure."

"Within a few minutes the tentative diagnosis from my electrocardiogram and the events that had occurred indicated that I had Ventricular Tachycardia. So, on advice from the ER, the EMS team started me on an intravenous medication to stop the V-Tach. Within a short while after that, maybe around 10 minutes I would say, I began to become alert and started feeling a little better, even being able to talk and move my arms and legs some."

"Thankfully, and miraculously for me, we arrived at the Hospital within a half hour and my heart rate was back in normal rhythm, controlled by the medication. Hey Victor, help me get another sip of water, would you?"

Victor got up from his bedside chair and said: "Sure Otto. Take it easy on yourself. I don't want to wear you out. You have had a hard couple days and another procedure coming tomorrow!"

Otto said: "Thanks for the water. I feel relatively relaxed right now, with some pain medication they gave me. Anyway, they did more blood studies, then sent me for a Cardiac catheterization to see if I had a heart attack. My coronary vessels were all open and no evidence of a clot or heart muscle damage."

"Next, they decided to continue my evaluation yesterday afternoon, so I was taken for a cardiac electrophysiology study. As you know, that required catheters in my femoral artery and vein, and inserting wires that could find any spots in my heart's electrical pathways that might be misfiring. They easily found two irritable sites in the ventricle and ablated them to stop their extra activity. There were several other irritable sites, but the Cardiac Electrophysiologist decided that there were too many to attempt any more ablations. So they stopped that procedure and scheduled me for an indwelling Pacemaker/Defibrillator placement. That procedure is occurring early tomorrow morning. That's the story Victor. I am probably exhausted and will sleep very well tonight."

Victor noted that although Otto was anxious and probably in some pain despite medications, his heart monitor tracings had been quite stable through all of this conversation.

Victor said: "Otto, I am glad your coronary arteries are clear and that you did not have a heart attack. However, Ventricular Tachycardia episodes can sometimes lead to ventricular fibrillation and death, as you know. The procedure in the morning sounds necessary and is the appropriate one. That and your anti- arrhythmic medications should keep you stable."

"My good friend, I don't want to bother you anymore tonight. I am just glad to see you. If it is agreeable with you, I will try to come back tomorrow evening and we can talk some more. Maybe you could try to think of ways I can help you out as you get ready to be discharged and get back to your home. Your daughter will probably also be able to come and help out a couple days. Otto, you should try and get some rest. I'll see you again tomorrow. OK?"

Otto, settling into a more relaxed position and in a rather quiet voice said: "Victor, thanks for dropping by. I look forward to seeing you again tomorrow. Take care of yourself. Say 'Hi' to Ruth from me next time you talk to her."

Victor said he certainly would do so.

Then, winking to Otto and with a little smile, said: "Otto, don't be too tough on the Nurses here." Otto smiled, getting Victor's semi-joking needling point, as Victor was leaving the room.

***

It was nearing darkness when Victor drove up his driveway. As usual, the steers headed along the pasture fence up to the feed bunker, expecting an evening grain ration. After parking, Victor first let Shadow out of the kennel to run free, yet staying within earshot of his master's voice. Victor left his briefcase on the porch steps, went to the feed shed for a bucket of grain and fed the steers. He then went into the house, Shadow following to the porch, also expecting to be fed.

Victor changed into a comfortable sweatshirt and jeans. He fed Shadow and allowed him to stay outside to stretch his legs some more. Victor took out a bowl of left over stir fry, containing chicken breast chunks, to warm in the microwave. He then poured himself a glass of wine. When the stir-fry was ready, Victor let Shadow back into the house to hang out on his pad by the door.

After eating, Victor took his bowl to the kitchen and rinsed it out. He then took his phone from the charger, sat down with his glass of wine, and dialed Ruth.

Ruth had caller ID and answered as soon as she could get to the phone: "Vic. I was so hoping you would call! I have missed you already, and it has only been two days."

Victor said: "Hi Ruth, I am feeling very lonely myself, and thinking of you obviously. Please tell me something of your day, or anything, just so I can enjoy your voice for a while."

Ruth replied: "I'd love to talk to you so long as I feel you are thinking of me instead of another nasty Committee Meeting."

Victor said: "Come on Ruth, I'll tell you about the meeting later. You can be sure I am totally thinking of you right now."

Ruth started: "Well, when I got home yesterday, I was tired and still thinking of the good time I had with you on the weekend. So I went to bed early and had no trouble falling asleep. Up at 5:30 this morning and to work on time. The hospital had gotten along just fine without me, and that was no surprise."

"I went on rounds with 2 different Cancer Care teams, hearing about new admissions, and learning of the present condition of patients I was previously involved with."

"After rounds, I went to meet with my supervisor. In addition to talking about work, she asked about our week-end together. I then started the day with my Pediatric patient assignments, and soon the work day was finished. I stopped at the Rec Center on the way home and had a good aerobic work-out. Now home, just put a casserole in the oven for my dinner, hoping you would call. And you did!"

Victor replied: "It sounds like you had a pretty good day overall. Now I'll take my turn and catch you up on things here at Lake View."

"First of all, some news about Otto Zellers. Later in the evening after we left his place, he had a cardiac event. EMS response was prompt. At the hospital, cardiac catheterization studies found no arterial blockage. Cardiac electrophysiology studies, however, found several sites of aberrant conduction. They ablated a couple, but decided there were too many irritable sites to continue that, so they stopped ablation attempts and scheduled him for an indwelling Pacemaker/Defibrillator placement tomorrow. So, Otto had a significant event of Ventricular Tachycardia, and fortunately he is stable now."

"I saw him briefly this evening. He seems to have tolerated the procedures reasonably well, but it was an exhausting experience for him."

Ruth responded: "Oh, he seemed like such a nice person and your good friend. I hope he gets through all this OK."

Victor said: "I plan to go see him again tomorrow evening and talk some more with him. I'll tell Otto you are thinking about him and are sending your best wishes. By the way, he says Hi to you."

"On the upside of the day, we received word from ICCPF that they awarded us a grant to help fund the Nanosphere Complex clinical study. They are also adding to the grant some support money for our new breast cancer bone metastases research. So, we were very happy with that news."

"Otherwise, the Committee meeting today was fairly frustrating. We talked about and clarified some details of the clinical study. That part went well. However, there were two issues that really bothered me."

"Dr. Green had invited Mike Jones from Lake View's financial office. To make a long story short, Lake View is taking more money out of all of the Faculty's research grant awards. This money will be used to help salary payments for unfunded Faculty. This is the brain child of a new Lake View Committee called, 'The Faculty Equity Committee'.

Now the deduction will be 10% of the grant awards that come from private foundations and pharmaceutical companies. Lake View is also trying to get more 'Indirect Costs' from Federal grant awards to help finance this Faculty Equity idea. However, that has not been agreed to by the Government as yet. I spoke strongly against both the financial and philosophical issues of this action."

Ruth said: "Oh Vic, I hope more Faculty speak out against this new plan. You work too hard on obtaining research funding to be taken advantage of like this. Of course, I might not know enough about the issues to comment. Maybe I am on your side just because we are lovers. What do you think?"

Victor said: "I am glad you are on my side, especially for the second reason you mentioned. Now, here is the other issue that concerned me about the meeting. I told the Committee about our recent work with breast cancer bone metastases as I discussed in the recent ICCPF application and award. I thought that both David Green and Jerry Smith got really upset by that information. I know they are doing research on breast cancer, but their work is focused on the cause and onset of breast cancer, not bone metastases. I tried to make that point to them, but I think they were quite angry with me that our lab was now studying breast cancer bone metastases."

Ruth, with a disappointed tone in her voice, responded: "Well Vic, remember that research was your original idea, and your lab did the hard work leading to your discovery. So, you just have to forget about their opinion and keep working hard on the project and see if the data and experiments confirm your early encouraging results. Don't let Green and Smith discourage you. Don't let them get into your project or try to steal any aspects of it from you. They might even try to discredit your new work on the breast cancer metastasis project. Vic, watch your back on this one."

Victor said: "Thanks, Ruth, for your support of me with all these issues I have going here. Now, what do you say we switch to talking about something else?"

Ruth spoke up quickly: "Vic, there is something I wanted to follow up on that you mentioned this past weekend. It also is a lighter subject than Committee meetings and work."

"This was about those novels you have been reading by an author named Tony Hillerman. You said the settings of those books were in the Southwest. So, I thought it might be interesting and beneficial for me to read a couple of those books. It would make me feel closer to you, reading some of the same books as you have read. Also, after all, I am down here in Phoenix in a Southwestern state."

Victor said: "Yes, I did mention this to you when you were here and am glad you are interested. For the past few years I have been reading, and just finished all the novels by Tony Hillerman. I would describe his novels as mostly crime mystery and action. His principal literary good guys are members of the Navajo Nation Tribal Police. These novels contain much about Navajo religion, superstitions, beliefs, occasionally Native American sovereignty issues, some historical glimpses of the various tribes or families in the Nation, and so on."

"I think Hillerman was pretty familiar with his subject matter. He apparently had certain connections with the Navajo Nation, and he lived in Albuquerque when writing his novels. His writings have been of interest to me for a couple of good reasons. One, I learned about some of the Navajo culture. Another interest was the Western setting of the Four Corners Region. Most of the Nation's land is in Northeast AZ and Northwest NM, with some in Southeast UT and a small chunk of Southwest CO."

"Hillerman regularly captures and describes the various Southwest landscapes and seasons. His appreciation of natural wonders of the region fits very well with my feelings about mountains and other of Earth's surface that I had talked with you about last weekend. He can take something like 'Shiprock', a remnant of an old volcano, still rising almost 1600 feet above the high desert plain in San Juan County, NM, and develop a mystery novel around it. Doing this, he brings out certain cultural aspects of the Navajo people. For example, 'Shiprock', or 'Rock with Wings' to the Navajo, has religious and historical significance for them. Anyway, his writing opened for me an interest in the Southwest cultures, traditions and its natural sights. I hope to get out to that region to see some of the landscape and landmarks sometime."

'Ruth said: "Vic, I can see you getting hooked on this author, and appreciating his knowledge and understanding of the land in that area. Maybe you would send me a couple of those novels for me to read and see how I like them."

Victor responded: "Ruth, I certainly will do that. Also, maybe the next time I visit you in Phoenix we can take a few days and drive up to see some of the area. Let's think of possibly doing that."

"Speaking of the next time I see you, let me tell

you something very serious. Ruth, I have been realizing that I really miss you very much. I want more and more to live with you, sleep with you, and be with you each day. I know we talked some about this already and the fact that right now might not be a good time, many things to consider, etc. But, maybe we could discuss moving up the timetable, what do you think of that?"

Ruth paused for a short while, then said: "Vic, I am feeling the same way about you. My work is important to me, but I am realizing that I can be a Pediatric Oncology Nurse not only in Phoenix, but at other sites as well. I could work at Lake View for example, or anywhere you might choose to go. Let's hope you soon have resolution of the issues surrounding your study and research funding. Then I will give notice to leave here, and apply for a job at the Lake View Hospital Pediatric Oncology unit. If that works out, we can start living with each other and make some plans together for our lives going forward."

Victor, a little surprised but very pleased, said: "Ruth, this sounds great! This week or so will be a crusher, but hopefully it will indicate to me a lot about what I can or cannot accomplish here at Lake View. On the other hand, it might lead me to think about moving my research program. You will be a great help in discussing options."

Ruth and Victor talked a while longer. Both were excited about this new step, even without knowing yet the timing or more details of their decision. After another half hour or so, they said goodnight and hung up their phones.   In bed, both were awake for another hour or so before falling asleep, thinking of one another.

13

Waking the next morning, Victor was excited remembering his telephone call with Ruth last night. He thought of that all through his shower and breakfast, fighting the urge to call her before he went to work. However, she would be busy getting to work herself, so he did not call.

Moritz's first objective this morning was going to the lab to see if there was any activity recorded overnight on the Trail Camera. After the usual morning routine with Shadow and the steers, he started for Lake View.

Moritz arrived before any other of his lab members. The first thing he did was to take a good look around after entering the lab. It was obvious that the Red Star Notebook had been moved further down on the lab bench from where he had left it last night. The camera on the shelf did not appear to have been disturbed. Moritz took the camera and went into the lab office. He removed the SD card from the camera and inserted it into the computer. He began to scan to see if any images were recorded.

The first part of the video showed Moritz leaving the lab last night. The camera video next showed that at 10:00 PM, the lab door had opened, the overhead lights came on as usual, and two members of the night cleaning crew entered. Over the next few minutes, they swept the floors between the lab benches and emptied the lab's trash cans into their larger containers. They then left the lab in a matter of 20 minutes.

The next images on the computer started at 11:25 PM. Moritz was not too surprised to see Jerry Smith come through the door into the laboratory. Jerry had paused, letting his eyes adjust to the lights that came on. He took a brief look around and then walked to the Red Star Notebook that was laying in plain sight on the first bench. Jerry moved the notebook down the bench a few feet where the lighting must have seemed better. He then started turning pages and paused occasionally to read some of the entries. At 11:45 PM, he looked at the front pages of the notebook that contained an Index. After apparently finding a section of special interest to him, Jerry took his cell phone and snapped pictures of several pages. At 12:05 AM, Jerry closed the notebook, put his cell phone back in his pocket, and left the laboratory, after which the lights went out again.

The final video frames had recorded Moritz coming in this morning.

Dr. Li Chen arrived at the lab as Moritz was finishing watching the video. After she had taken off her jacket and put on her lab coat, Moritz said: "Li, come over and sit a couple minutes please. I have something to show you. See if you can identify anything in this video. I would like to know if you see what I have seen."

Dr. Chen came over and sat down beside Moritz in front of the computer screen. Moritz then started a video replay from the beginning. He said: "Let's watch a few minutes and then I will stop the video and ask you what you saw."

Moritz skipped the part of his leaving the lab and then started the recording. After the 20 minutes of the cleaning crew, Moritz stopped the video and asked: "OK, Li, tell me what you saw here."

Li said: "I clearly saw a video of the cleaning crew enter and clean in our laboratory, at the usual time they come each Tuesday, Thursday, and Saturday evenings, right around ten o'clock. Sometimes I am still working when they arrive."

Moritz said: "Could you see any face that looked familiar to you? Were the images clear enough to identify someone? Did you see where the Red Star Notebook was on the lab bench?"

Li responded: "I recognized both of the cleaning team. The tall one is named Atlee, the one with the beard is Denver. I don't know their last names, but I clearly recognized them. The Red Star Notebook is laying on the lab bench where I left it when talking to you yesterday evening, roughly 5-6 feet from the end of the first bench."

Moritz said: "OK, let's look at some more video and again please tell me what you see this time."

Moritz started the video again and let it play until it finished. He then turned off the computer and looked at Dr. Chen. He said: "Li, what did you see on this part of the video?"

Li cried out: "Oh my God! I saw Dr. Jerry Smith enter our laboratory. He saw the Red Star Notebook and moved it down the bench for better lighting, and started going through the pages for a few minutes. He then apparently looked at the Index at the beginning of the notebook. After that, he began to look at specific pages. Some of these pages he photographed using his cell phone, then he left the lab. The last pictures in the video showed you coming into the lab this morning."

Li looked at the Trail Camera on the desk beside the computer, and pointed at it while looking at Moritz.   She nodded at him with a smile of approval.

Both Victor and Li were quiet for a few minutes, reviewing their thoughts before speaking about what they had just witnessed.

Moritz said: "So, Li, we have this and the previous unfriendly visit with you in our lab by Dr. Green and Jerry. I am going to use these two incidents to be sure, but exactly how I have not decided yet. I think, as a minimum, these two Faculty members should be disqualified from having a vote at the Committee that is reviewing my proposed clinical study protocol. I am thinking I will put an exclamation mark on this issue by revealing the situation to both the Director of Science and the Chairman of the Department of Oncology. There should be some Faculty discipline. The photographing and stealing of data from our notebook should haunt Jerry Smith's credibility for years."

Li said: "I agree with you. Such unethical behavior as we have seen here is totally out of line. I just hope that these two Committee members do not have a mechanism, or certain ties with Lake View Administrators, that will allow them to get back at you, and me, in some way. Who would have ever thought we would have experienced what we have already been through. Who knows what will be next, the way some things are happening in this institution already." She shook her head with an exasperated expression on her face.

Moritz said: "Li, I will take this business forward, and will keep you in touch with what develops. Thanks for your patience. I hope the rest of your day is better than the scene I presented you when you walked in this morning."

Then, with a smile on his face, Moritz said: "Hey, and don't forget to tell me about those new and secret experiments you and Mark are working on together, when you have some data."

By this time, Mark and Charlie had arrived in the lab to start work. Dr. Chen nodded to Moritz and then went to her work bench and started to prepare for experiments of the day. Moritz greeted Mark and Charlie and asked about the lecture they attended yesterday. However, he did not show them the video. He then returned to his computer, made a copy of the video, and saved it. He removed the original SD card, and put it in a small envelope which he put in his jacket pocket. Moritz told his lab team to have a good day and he headed for patient rounds on the ward.

***

During patient rounds, Moritz received a phone Text from Dr. Green's office saying that his Committee was meeting again tomorrow afternoon for final comments, appraisal, and vote on his clinical study proposal. Mike Jones of the financial office would be attending the meeting again, and would have voting privileges the same as the other members of the Committee.

After receiving that Text from Green's office, Moritz had called the Director of Science's Office to see if the Director was available to meet with him sometime tomorrow morning. Moritz told the Director's Administrative Assistant that the purpose of the meeting would be to review the progress of the Committee evaluating his clinical research study. It so happened that the Director was available at 10:00 AM, and he would welcome a meeting with Dr. Moritz tomorrow morning.

After patient rounds and a lunch break, Dr. Moritz spent the afternoon seeing his clinic patients.

During a break in the clinic patient schedule, Moritz had called the Cardiac ward to ask about Otto Zellers. The Nurse said he had the indwelling Pacemaker successfully placed at 7:00 AM and that he returned to his ward room from the recovery area at about 11:00 AM. Presently he was awake and doing well. He would be able to see Dr. Moritz this evening for an hour between 7:00 and 9:00 PM. Moritz asked her to please tell Otto that he would be in at 7:00 to visit for a while, and thanked her for the information and help.

Dr. Moritz spent the remainder of the late afternoon and early evening in his clinic office. He finished notes electronically on the clinic patients he had seen in the afternoon. He also thought about the call he had received from Jim Davis that afternoon.

Jim had called to ask if he could possibly be helpful to Moritz by attending the next Committee meeting. Jim said he was feeling somewhat improved. He, with Rita's help, could attend a meeting and briefly make a statement supporting the clinical study if Moritz thought it would help. Moritz had returned Jim's call. Although there was the short notice of the meeting called for tomorrow afternoon, Jim said he could be there. Moritz had agreed. Jim and he decided that Jim would say a few words about his own prostate cancer bone metastases and why he would like to see Dr. Moritz's protocol pass as an option for terminal patients like himself. He would urge that the study start as soon as possible. Then he would leave the meeting.

While in his office, Moritz also took some time making a few notes on how he was going to approach the meeting tomorrow after Jim's comments. First, probably a couple of short review points of their progress in the lab. Then he would again stress the need for a new cure approach for people in Jim's condition. He also planned to present his comments on Green and Smith's visit to the lab, harassing Dr. Chen. Finally, he would show the video of Jerry's lab intrusion, before the voting took place. He was not sure of the effect of bringing everyone up to date on these ethical issues, but it seemed to be the time to speak up.

***

It was another Hospital Deli for Moritz's evening meal. He ate at a table in the Deli with some Oncology Residents who were on call this night and happened to be eating at the same time.

Moritz arrived on the Cardiac Unit promptly at 7:00 PM. The Nurse said Otto had a good long nap this afternoon and had finished a soft diet meal an hour ago. Monitoring of heart rate, blood pressure, oxygenation and electrocardiogram had been satisfactory. He had been switched to oral anti-arrhythmic and pain medications. The last intravenous access would be discontinued in the morning. After that, he would receive instructions on the care of his wound where the recent Pacemaker/Defibrillator was implanted in his upper left chest. He would also be given instructions on using the wireless recording monitor at home. That monitor could send his Pacemaker device data to the Cardiac electrophysiology team at regular intervals to follow his condition.

Otto was expecting Victor and smiled when Victor came in. An easy handshake today, but you could tell they were glad to see each other.

Otto said: "Nice to see you again Victor. Pull up a chair closer to my bed, if you would, so we can talk easier."

Otto reviewed what he remembered of the implant procedure. The Medical and Nursing staffs had been very good in explaining everything about the procedure to him.

Otto said: "The long and short of it is that I have a data recorder and a battery box sewed to my chest muscle under the skin. There are two wires coming from this Pacemaker box, one goes to my right ventricle and the other goes to the right atrium. The Pacemaker fires a signal down these wires if my heart rate is too slow, too fast, or is not in a regular rhythm. Minor electrical impulses will not be noticeable. However, if the recording Pacemaker/Defibrillator needs to make a heavy discharge to correct a life threatening heart rate pattern, like fibrillation, there would be a moment of significant sharp pain in my chest from the defibrillating electrical shock."

"If I have a good night tonight, they plan to discharge me tomorrow sometime."

Victor said: "Is your daughter going to be able to arrive in time tomorrow to help you get home and settled in?"

Otto said: "Yes, Amy left her place driving this morning. She will stay in a motel on the road tonight and arrive here about noon tomorrow. She plans on staying a few days, buying groceries, cooking and freezing some meals for me, being sure I am stable, taking my medication correctly, and so forth. Then she will drive back to her home and family and hopefully will get back to her work next week."

"Amy told me over the phone that I ought to consider selling my house here in the Lake View area and move closer to her, her husband and my two grandchildren. I told her that all my friends and routines are around here, so I will try to keep hanging out in my familiar area for as long as I am able. She didn't sound too disappointed with that, but it's hard to tell on the phone."

"I think I told you before that Amy's husband does not seem to like me particularly well. I am not sure if it is about some specific event or reason. More likely it is because I know he is an in your face liberal. He knows I have pretty conservative leanings, and don't like his politics. He also knows I don't like his attempts at lecturing me on politics when all I would like to do is play the 'Old Maid' card game with my grandchildren. Anyway, let's leave that subject alone and not take up any more of your visitor time with it."

Victor said: "Well Otto, I am glad Amy can be here for a few days, and get you re-settled in your home. I want to help you out if I can, but it happens that the next couple days are going to be pretty busy. I am tied up with meetings and head butting about my clinical study. Also, there is new business in the Lake View financial office that I talked to you about the other day. They are now taking more money from awarded research grants. That increased revenue will be targeted for new Administrative ventures such as 'Faculty Equity' pay."

Otto readjusted his pillow and pushed the control button to raise the head of his bed a little more, and said: "Yes, I remember you told me about that development."

Victor thought about it, but did not bring up the subject of Jerry Smith's entry into the lab last night, and the video of the event.

Instead, Victor changed the subject and

continued: "But Otto, let me quit talking about this Committee business for now. After Amy returns to her family, I want to try to help you adjusting to life back in your own home. I could do things like stop by each evening after my work in the lab or hospital. Maybe we could talk a little together. Or maybe you would need something from the store that I could shop for and bring to you. You will probably not feel like attempting to drive for a few weeks."

"I could bring in the mail and newspaper on some bad weather days, bring in a meal for you from the Deli, or check with you that you are taking your medications correctly. Maybe you have some ideas of how I can help out. I know you enjoy being independent, and I don't mean to push you. I am just more than willing to help out if and when I can. So Otto, at least think about it."

Otto said: "Victor, I certainly do appreciate such an offer from you. I probably will need some help for a while with a few of the things you mentioned. I have arranged to have the household cleaning service come twice a week, instead of every other week, for the next six weeks, so that will also help. Let's see how it goes. However, to start with, after Amy has left please stop by each evening after work for a few days. When I gain some strength back and have confidence returning with my daily routines, you won't need to come so often."

***

Victor answered: "Otto, I will enjoy stopping in. Maybe some days I will be a little later than others, but you can be sure I will be showing up. You know, Otto, I look at you as one of my very best friends."

"Also, as I have told you before, you remind me a lot of my late Father. Like you, he tried to be as independent as he could be, and yet respect the rights and feelings of others."

"Dad was fair and trusting of a hard- working and honest person. Like you, right? I know you used to give credit and occasionally delay payment deadlines of some financially struggling patients in your medical practice. For the most part, I'll bet their bill was eventually paid through their efforts. Dad would do this at his gasoline service station business. He would run a credit tab for someone who might have been temporally down on their luck, but was honest and trying to work through their situation. These relatively minor debtors would usually stop in each week, or when they could, and pay a few dollars on their bill. Gradually they almost always paid off the full amount they had charged. He had a knack of trusting the right

216

person."

"Otto, I also know you as usually a calm and soft spoken man. Yet, I have seen you get up at a Faculty meeting and defend someone who was taking an unnecessary, and maybe untrue, amount of criticism from other members in the meeting. I have always admired that in you.

"Again, just like you, Dad was not an argumentative person for the sake of arguing. However, he would speak out at times."

"I can remember one time when I was a child and heard Dad speak up strongly. There was a man in my home town that made his meager living expenses doing different seasonal odd jobs. For example, when in season, Jake would buy elderberries from people in the area that had picked small amounts, like a bushel or so. Jake would accumulate large amounts and then would resell to some other place, like a grocery store chain, or a jelly factory.   He also did other seasonal enterprises like buying and selling roots and animal furs to make a livable income."

"Jake was older, somewhat unsteady at times, but still drove his midsize pick-up truck as needed for his projects. One day, Jake was hauling a load of elderberries and collided with another vehicle at a 4-way stop. This accident occurred on the corner of town where Dad's gasoline service station was located. Of course, a crowd gathered at the site of the collision. Fortunately, neither driver was seriously hurt. Jake was jarred some with the impact, and had just remained sitting in his truck, still in the middle of the intersection. While waiting for the town's Marshall to arrive at the scene, a couple persons talked to Jake to be sure he was OK, as well as the other driver. Almost everyone in town liked Jake. Despite his being poor, he always was trying to make a living and take care of himself. The truck was stalled, but the damage was limited to the passenger side door and cargo space on that side. The load of elderberries was not damaged."

"While Jake was still shaking a little and not yet ready to get out of his truck, one of the town's more affluent and full of himself business men came over to Jake's side of the truck, and started shouting criticisms at him. Although it was not yet established that Jake and his old truck were the cause of accident, Harry was blaming Jake for the collision. Harry kept saying to Jake that he was regularly a poor driver, and that it was about time something like this had happened to him. Harry kept on about it repeatedly."

"In the middle of Harry's criticism of Jake and his

driving, my Dad stepped up and spoke to Harry. He said, in words that I remember to this day. 'Harry, this is a Hell of a poor time to be telling Jake about your opinion, and criticizing him. He is obviously shaken up and doesn't need this right now'. Two or three people in the small crowd shouted, 'Yes, we agree, back off Harry.' Harry then turned on Dad and told him to mind his own business, unless he wanted to do something about it. Dad shrugged off Harry's finger pressed into his chest and told Harry again his concern on the timing of this criticism of Jake. By this time, Marshall Hyatt had arrived on the scene. He stepped between Harry and Dad, spoke to them briefly, then turned his attention to Jake and the other driver and began getting at the particulars of the accident. In a few minutes, everyone drifted off, Harry and Dad in opposite directions, never to be friends again from that day forward."

Otto said: "Victor, it sounds like your Dad was a straight up man with some spine. You must have been especially proud of him on that day."

Victor responded: "Yes, Otto, that is true. But you know, I didn't express that respect and pride of him to his face very often. I know I didn't say it directly. Maybe I beat around the bush with a compliment here or there. I wish I would have told him more often how proud of him I always was. I regret not doing so."

"There are other things I am also ashamed of in regards to Dad. Once, he and Mom decided that he was going to buy and start wearing a gold chain around his neck. This was when he was around 75 years old. When I visited Mom and Dad once around that time, I made some sort of negative remark about the necklace. I don't remember exactly my comment, but it was rude. Whatever I said affected him negatively, I am sure of that. The next time I visited, he was not wearing the gold chain and I never saw it on him again. Otto, I felt so bad about this. To make matters worse, I never apologized for making such a negative comment about his necklace. I hurt his feelings, I never forgot this incident, and felt bad about it frequently as time went by. I know some men wear necklaces. I do not know why I was so negative. Anyway, this is one occasion I cannot forgive myself over."

"Another incident with my Dad that I truly regret is about my beard. Dad never seemed to like my having a beard after I became a Physician. He had sported a mustache for a few years himself. However, he didn't think it was professional, or not fashionable, for me to have a beard. One day when he brought this up, it got me particularly angry, and I spoke out at him. I said I was not ever going to shave my beard off. Then I said, 'Not even for your funeral.' Otto, can you imagine that! I am so sorry I said that. This still haunts me. I remember the look on his face after my spouting off. I hope he swore at me under his breath, but he was probably looking ahead and was forgiving me."

"I am so sorry I did not immediately apologize to him for these two inappropriate and bitter comments of mine. I hope he was able to forgive my stupidity before his passing. I should have asked his forgiveness directly, but I never did. I was not able to be at his bedside when he was dying to say how sorry I was. We had never talked about these things after they happened. I am still embarrassed and ashamed when I think about them."

Otto was paying close attention to Victor while he was talking. He noticed the remorse in Victor's face, and more than once a quiver in his voice, obviously trying not to cry. After a pause, Otto reached out, and opening the palm of his hand in Victor's direction, said: "Victor, I know from past conversations we have had regarding your Father that you two loved each other and had a very solid Father-Son relationship."

"A close relationship wasn't easy all the time. He was working 12-14 hour days running your family's gas service station business when you were in Grade and High School. Even so, he did try his best to make it to your High School basketball and football games. He often closed the business early so he could come and see a couple innings of the summer league softball team you played on. You worked in the garden together and you helped out a lot working at the gas station."

"Then you left town for college, then Graduate and Medical Schools, then Medical and Oncology Residencies, then a Faculty position. None of these experiences were close to where your parents lived. All those years and many miles separating you two. Not seeing your Mother was additionally hard as well, I am sure."

"You wrote letters and talked on the phone frequently. You almost always visited twice a year and spent time talking, playing euchre and having a beer or working together when possible. Overall, you did a great job with the relationship with your Dad. Sure, you made a few blunders that I am certain hurt him at the time, but who is perfect? My guess is that your Dad's final thoughts when passing were first of your Mother, and immediately after, he thought of how proud of you he was.

Take it easy on yourself, Victor."

"If you regard me as having some traits, habits, or ideology that reminds you of your Father, this gives me great pleasure. Now, let me lay something on you. To tell the truth, I often think of you as what I would have wished for if my wife and I had a Son. I would be so proud of you if you were my Son. So, it seems with this issue that we are on the same page. I am happy with that."

Victor said: "Me too, and thanks Otto."

The hour had gone by quickly. The nurse returned to Otto's room and checked the monitor readings. All were still satisfactory. However, she felt that Otto was looking a little washed out and probably would be helped by having a snack and getting some sleep. She told both Otto and Dr. Moritz her assessment and asked them what they thought.

Both Otto and Victor told her they thought she was right in her judgement. So, Victor and Otto said their goodnights, and wished each other well, promising to see one another in a couple days after Otto was settled back in his home.

Victor thanked the Nurse and Clerk as he left the ward. He then headed to his car in the parking lot.

14

Victor Moritz was up early again the following morning. After completing his personal and chore routines with the animals, he started on the road to Lake View by 6:00 AM.

In the lab office, Moritz first reviewed and made notes on what he wanted to present to the Director of Science. He then studied again the video from the Trail Camera and wrote down several comments he might want to speak about.

After Dr. Chen arrived for work, the two of them reexamined the expected expenses of the research program for the next 5 years. This included the research laboratory expenses, support for the clinical study, and salaries for Moritz, Chen, and a Graduate Student position presently occupied by Mark. Then they factored in the percent that Lake View planned to additionally take for the new 'Indirect Costs' requirement, which included the Faculty Equity Committee's program. Calculations showed that, even with the addition of the recent grant from the ICCPF, they would have to find ways to cut back on some planned experiments. However, Moritz again reassured Dr. Chen that her salary and performance raises for the next 5 years were solid commitments and adequately funded.

Moritz also shared with her that he had recently contacted several other potential private charitable endowments designated for cancer studies. He had already received favorable responses from three of these endowments saying they would contribute to his proposed clinical study, pending approval by the Committee at Lake View.

By the time Moritz and Chen had finished their budget review, it was 9:40 AM. Chen wished Dr. Moritz luck with today's Committee meeting, then went to work in the lab, along with Mark, who had arrived while she was talking with Moritz. Moritz finished organizing his notes and made certain he had the copy of the Trail Camera video with him. He put the video copy and his notes into a zippered portfolio, closed his desk and left the office. Leaving the lab, he greeted Mark, and told him and Dr. Chen to have a good day. He then set out for the office of the Director of Science at Lake View.

***

The receptionist at the Science Director's office warmly welcomed Dr. Moritz when he arrived five minutes early. She offered him a cup of coffee or water, which he declined. She then buzzed the Director on the intercom.

Director Stan Wright opened his office door,

greeted Moritz, and invited him in. The Director stood at six feet four inches, had broad shoulders, and a slim frame. Prominent cheek bones helped accent his warm greeting smile. Moritz and Stan Wright had a firm respectful handshake. The Director's blazer was hanging on the back of his desk chair. This and his loosened necktie gave a somewhat more relaxed feeling to the room, which was helpful in calming Moritz's nerves.

Moritz had known Dr. Stan Wright since Wright had accepted the Director's position at Lake View three years ago. Most of their interactions, however, were in group settings such as when, twice a year, the Director attended the Department of Oncology's Faculty meetings.

Moritz thanked Director Wright for taking the time to see him. Director Wright then asked Moritz to have a seat as he settled himself behind his desk.

Wright opened the conversation: "It is good to see you Victor. I am somewhat acquainted with your productive work here at our Center. Just today, I received word about your recent grant awarded by the ICCPF. Congratulations for that. Your research, teaching, and clinical work have made an excellent impression on those of us in the science administrative positions here at Lake View.

Now, what is on your mind today?"

Moritz spent a few minutes reviewing his research program and his emphasis on prostate cancer metastases to bone. He then described his clinical research study proposal that was presently before the 'Patient Care and Research Ethics Committee'. He also summarized the first two Committee meetings. He noted of being informed in the second meeting of the additional financial requirements coming from the Financial Office that were presented by Michael Jones. Moritz included the announcement of the use of some grant money for the new Faculty Equity Committee. Moritz told Director Wright of how he had voiced strong opinions against the plans of taking more research dollars for Administrative uses and the Faculty Equity Committee.

Director Wright had listened carefully to Moritz. He now spoke up: "Yes Victor, I was aware that this movement was happening in the Financial Department. Personally, I feel that increasing the percent of grant money taken for Administrative expenses, the 'Indirect Costs,' should be increased somewhat. Overhead costs for the Hospital, library, emergency room, clinical facilities and so forth have risen noticeably the last few years. Some of that is due to the increase generally in the cost of living. Some of it is also due to ever increasing mandates and regulations required to keep our Hospital and Medical Training programs in compliance with National and State guidelines. We must abide by these in order to keep our institution accredited and functioning."

"However, Victor, I spoke against two items during those Financial Department deliberations. First, I thought the suggested overhead withdrawal from new grants of 10% was too high and should be closer to 7.5%. Secondly, I generally thought formation of a Faculty Equity Committee was not a good idea. I spoke directly against how they planned to use the newly levied money to approach balance of all Faculty salaries. I commented about the potential effects on the scientific efforts of our Faculty. Specifically, I worry that at least some Faculty will become complacent and less competitive in Science and productive research. I am afraid that will hurt the credibility and mission of our Lake View Medical Center. So I am with you on that point Victor. What else is on your mind?"

Victor moved forward in his chair, and looking straight into the Director's eyes, began: "Today is the 3rd Committee Meeting. The plan is to vote on my clinical study proposal. At the first meeting of this Committee, I felt strongly that two of the members were not interested in allowing my study to go forward. I am not sure why. Scientifically, the work is very sound. The support by the NCI and FDA to go forward with a clinical study is strong. I feel my proposal is supported by three of the Committee members. The others that are likely against my study seem to have something personal against me or maybe there is professional jealously involved."

"It could maybe even be anger towards me because of some of my conservative and individual rights views and opinions that I speak out for from time to time. In any event, this animosity towards me, and my worry of the rejection of the study, has gone far beyond discussing just scientific and factual issues by the Committee."

"Let me give you some background on why I say this. Before the first Committee meeting, Dr. David Green and Dr. Jerry Smith went to my laboratory and intimidated and verbally harassed my Postdoctoral Fellow, Dr. Li Chen. After a few minutes of conversation, they became rude and downright disrespectful toward her. For example, they said there must be some important negative findings in our research results, and asked to see laboratory notes confirming this. When Dr. Chen told them the lab results had consistently fully supported our working hypothesis and supported our proposed clinical study, they tried to distort her answers and trick her into certain other false statements, scoffing and intimidating her. When Dr. Chen held her own during this questioning, they began another approach."

"These Committee members also offered her bonus money or an academic scientific promotion a year earlier than what she is expecting from me. She would only have to state, in writing, that she knew of negative results that would be detrimental for the whole project."

With a facial expression showing obvious surprise and amazement, Director Wright said: "My God, Victor, how can this have happened?"

Dr. Moritz continued: "Director Wright, there is more. You are beginning to understand why I asked for an appointment with you this morning."

"I did not bring up the actions of Green and Smith at the Committee Meetings as yet. At the second meeting that I told you briefly about a few minutes ago, Dr. Green announced that Mike Jones would have voting rights along with the original group of the Committee. So, I now began to suspect again that the Committee was being stacked against me."

"Maybe I was becoming paranoid about it, but I was suspicious of the situation. So, I decided to set a trap for my suspected anti-Moritz person, or persons. I set a video camera in our laboratory, and my hunch was verified. The video camera recorded a faculty member, Dr. Jerry Smith, at 11:25 PM, entering my lab."

"Dr. Smith looked through a lab notebook that was in plain sight on a lab benchtop. This lab notebook is specific for our recent research interest studying breast cancer bone metastases. We had labelled this as the 'Red Star Notebook'. In addition, he took pictures of a few pages of this notebook with his cell phone camera. About forty five minutes after entering the lab, Smith left, unaware of having been filmed."

Director Wright, now more astonished, asked: "Do you have a copy of this video that I can have to view later today? Victor, this is very serious. What is your plan for the meeting today when the vote is supposed to occur?"

Moritz said: "Well, Director Wright, I had planned to expose the whole business to the Committee. This includes the abuse of Dr. Chen, the invasion of the lab, and the theft of lab data by photographing some contents of our Red Star Notebook."

"I will argue that such actions against me, as a minimum, should disqualify Green and Smith from having legitimate votes on my proposed clinical study. This is the information I wanted you to hear about. I ask you, Director Wright, to consider if any other actions or sanctions, ought and could be, imposed by your office on these two Faculty members. After all, they are members of the Science and Oncology Divisions of Lake View. Can you help my situation in any way?"

Director Wright spoke: "Yes, Victor, I will try to help. This is serious unethical behavior, the most egregious I have seen or heard of since I took my position here three years ago. I agree that these two persons should not have influence in possibly disapproving of your proposed clinical study. They also should face other consequences for their actions. You know that I appointed the members of this Committee, since it is one of my functions as Director of Science. I never would have thought that such behavior would have occurred by a Committee that I appointed."

"Victor, I am completely in support of you. However, let me also be straight with you on how I must approach this. First, I will notify the Head of the Division of Oncology about the situation so you won't have to go through reviewing this business again, unless you desire to. I doubt that you would want to."

"Second, I am telling you that I am required to bring this to the President of our Lake View Medical Center. There are certain limits on what Division Directors are permitted to do in situations like this. For example, I could not just fire Green and Smith, even though I might want to. The President will clarify to me how far I might go with punishment or removal of members from your Committee. There are restrictions on discipline that only the President can decide to implement. Other restrictions are in place. For example, at this point in time, we cannot make your situation public, even to other members of the Faculty. So, I will get clear information on what my options are under the circumstances."

"Third, Dr. David Green has been at Lake View since the beginning of its Research and Medical School program, which came a few years after the Hospital first opened. He has many friends in and outside of the Lake View organization. Most of them support him almost without question. This is true even when his judgement or behavior is out of line, as it has been before. He also has protected Jerry Smith in the past when Jerry was in trouble. So, you know some of the situation we are facing

233

here. I am not sure how much influence Dr. Green has on the President."

"What time is your Committee meeting today?"

Moritz said: "It is scheduled for two o'clock. It usually starts pretty promptly."

'Director Wright said: "Victor, I don't know if I can get any answers or action plan put together by that time. However, I think you should go to the meeting and present your case as you have planned. See what the reactions are. Is there denial, admission of doing wrong, efforts to reconcile feelings between you, or what else? I will attempt to meet with the President as soon as he has time available. Please leave me a copy of the video to review. Believe me, Victor, I am going to get involved in this problem we have."

Getting up from his chair, Victor put a copy of the video on the Director's desk, saying: "Director Wright, I appreciate your seeing me this morning on such short notice. I will go to the meeting and continue the battle. Thank you for beginning the work with the President. Hopefully in the long run it will help get my clinical study approval. I look forward to hearing from you when you have some news."

Director Wright and Victor Moritz shook hands and Moritz left the office.

It was now a little after eleven o'clock and Victor, who had gotten up early this morning, needed some lunch. He bought a sandwich and tea at the Deli and went to his clinic office. Moritz had no clinic patients scheduled today, so he expected some quiet time before the meeting.

After finishing lunch, Moritz called Otto Zeller's room. Otto told Victor that his orientation regarding his implanted cardiac monitoring Pacemaker/Defibrillator went well this morning. Otto also received instructions to limit his arm and shoulder movements on the side of his chest where the implant had been placed. Then he should gradually increase use and movement over the next couple weeks. Finally, he was also informed, that by law, he was not to drive a car for three months. He complained about this to Victor.

Victor said: "That restriction is to be sure your cardiac Pacemaker/Defibrillator is working properly since you had a previous loss of consciousness episode with your cardiac arrhythmia."

Otto said he thought that three months was too long, but that he would comply. Then he reminded Moritz about the offer to help out with his recovery process. Otto gave a little chuckle over this reminder to Victor of the commitment.

Victor then began telling Otto about his meeting with Director Wright: "I went to the Director of Science today to explain my problems with the Committee. You already know about the Green and Smith harassment of Dr. Chen. I also have video evidence of Jerry Smith entering my lab in the middle of the night, when no one was around. He was looking through one of our lab notebooks. Director Wright seemed appropriately stunned that members of the Faculty here at Lake View would stoop so low. He will speak to the President about disciplinary options that might be possible for him to initiate."

Otto interrupted Victor's positive comments: "Victor, let me give you some advice. Be careful of the faith and trust you give to Director Wright and the President. I am sometimes a little surprised with how Administrators, Presidents and Directors come down on an issue. This is especially relevant in this Institution that seems to be undergoing some type of change in its ideology. You also mentioned the fact already of David Green's widespread support that Director Wright told you about. This could go a long way in protecting Green against any intimidation and harassment charges. It would be his word against that of Dr. Chen. Can you see who might come out on top there?"

"Also, you do not know if Dr. Green had anything to do with Jerry Smith's entering your lab, going through your notebook and taking pictures of personal lab data."

"Don't get me wrong, Victor. I sincerely hope you nail these unethical scum. Just don't set your hopes too high. Be happy if your clinical study is approved to start. This is something that you can then accomplish. Some of these accusation and punishment issues might take a while to be resolved, and might even not end to your satisfaction, despite all the information you have against them."

Victor recognized the potential truth in Otto's warnings against being too optimistic about the situation's outcome. It was something he also had thought about, despite hoping otherwise.

After a pause, Victor changed the topic of the conversation, saying: "Otto, has Amy arrived yet to help with your discharge and getting settled back in your home?"

Otto said: "Victor, you changed our previous conversation subject, but I don't blame you. Just stay on your toes so an Administrator or another Faculty group doesn't try to get back at you in some way."

"Yes, I heard from Amy about an hour ago. She was in a supermarket about 35 minutes from here, buying food items and some bandage supplies that we can use for the next few days. She plans to get here around one o'clock. I will be glad when she arrives. I want to get back home, as you can imagine. By the way, she said to say 'Hi" to you. I am sure she will have some suggestions, that is, instructions for us to follow as she leaves town and you will be looking in on me."

Otto continued speaking: "Now tell me Victor, have you talked with Ruth lately? I like that woman, even though I only met and talked with her once so far."

Victor said: "Yes, Otto, we had a great phone conversation lately. We talked about our mutual loving attraction for each other. We made the commitment to start thinking of ways that would get us living together, sooner rather than later. In part, this depends on Committee approval of my study. If that doesn't happen maybe we will start looking for different job sites. I would be looking for a position in a University Medical School Oncology Department, preferably in the Western USA."

"I certainly want a position where I could bring my research program and have a good chance of getting this Nanosphere Complex clinical study underway. Ruth also wants to have the opportunity of getting a Nursing position. We definitely want to live together sharing life's experiences instead of talking about them over the phone or other electronic methods. What do you think of that plan?"

Otto said: "Wow! Sounds like good progress for getting together. Naturally, I hope your protocol gets approved here at Lake View. If you moved, of course I would miss my best friend very much. In any event, I wish you and Ruth the best of luck in working all this out for your happiness together."

Victor answered: "Thanks Otto, I'll keep you up to date. I should hang up now as I need to review the things I want to say at this afternoon's meeting. Say 'Hi' to Amy for me when she arrives, and good luck as you gradually get back to enjoying your home."

Otto agreed that they should hang up and get on with their days. Afterwards, Victor used the next hour of quiet in his office to work on his approach to today's Committee meeting.

15

Dr. David Green opened the Committee meeting by advising the members that Mike Jones from the Financial office was attending the meeting again. He also stated that, as Committee chairman, it was his right to grant Mike Jones voting status on the clinical study protocol under consideration, which he has done. Green then turned to Dr. Moritz and asked him what further information he had to offer the Committee at this time.

Dr. Victor Moritz stood, said good afternoon to the now six Committee members, and started his comments: "First, I will remind Dr. Green that I notified his office that I was planning on a brief introduction of a patient, Jim Davis. Jim wants to say a few words in support of the proposed clinical study on treating prostate cancer bone metastases. After Jim is finished, we will try to answer any questions that his conversation might have brought up concerning the study. When Jim then leaves, I will try to answer any other questions that you might have thought of since our last meeting. Following that, I would like to present some final relevant material before there is a vote taken."

"I hope that is agreeable to you, Mr. Chairman, and other members of the Committee."

Green replied: "I am sure that your patient's

appearance will be acceptable to all of us, so long as it does not push too late into the afternoon. Go ahead and ask Jim to come in."

Moritz thanked Dr. Green, went to the door of the conference room and opened it. He greeted Rita and Jim, who were waiting in the hallway. Moritz motioned Rita through the door and followed her, pushing Jim in his wheel chair. Moritz introduced Rita and Jim to the Committee. He then positioned a chair for Rita at the conference table. Next, he wheeled Jim to the front of the table, next to Rita, and returned to his own seat, now on Jim's right

Moritz said: "Last week, Jim asked me if he could attend a meeting to say a few words about our proposed study. He thought the Committee should hear from someone who is hoping for a chance for a remission or cure for his metastatic bone cancer. Jim, you now have the opportunity to give us your statement and thoughts."

Jim Davis straightened himself in his wheelchair as much as he could manage. It was obvious to everyone around the table that he was in pain when trying to move his back or legs to position himself somewhat better in his chair. When he was attempting this, Rita had started to get up to help him. However, Jim waved her off with a smile and a raised hand that indicated to her that he was settled enough.

Jim began to speak: "Dr. Green, and members of this Committee, thank you for allowing me to say a few words."

"I was born and raised in this area of the State. At 20 years of age, I started a small bakery business that was, thankfully, successful and a good living for myself, Rita and our family. At the age of 50, my prostate cancer was diagnosed. Despite various therapeutic approaches with radiation, surgery, and chemotherapy, I have developed uncontrolled bone metastases in my legs and spine. I am sure you can tell this by my disabled appearance and limited movement. Rita has taken over any consulting needed by the new owners of our bakery business. She has also cared for me as I have gone through this cancer process for the past 4 years. Rita's love and support of my situation, experiencing swings of despair and hope and then despair again, are truly remarkable."

As Jim took a pause in speaking, he and Rita reached for and held each other's hand for a moment.

Then Jim went on talking: "Dr. Moritz has fought this cancer with me from the beginning. He utilized the time proven and recommended protocols, medications, and procedures. He tried new methods as they became available. He has consulted with experts throughout the world to determine if there were additional approaches to treat my metastatic bone condition. The recognition of his clinical expertise in fighting my cancer is a given, in my opinion."

"Beyond that, Dr. Moritz has, through his basic research studies, discovered a method to treat and cure prostate cancer bone metastases in experimental animals. Now, his goal is to see if his basic research discovery can be translated into actual human clinical care. Dr. Moritz has kept me fully informed of his proposed clinical study of using the Nanosphere Complex to attack my bone metastases. He has also kept Rita and I informed about the discussions and concerns that have occurred in this Committee."

"Members of the Committee, I am in palliative care and classified as terminal. I am there, and here with you, because I am hopeful of some new therapeutic approach to cure, or at least halt, any more effects from these metastatic cells that are destroying many of my bones."

"Yes, I am likely addicted to pain pills. One approach we could do is to increase the dose and I would die soon and with less pain. This is not for me. I would much rather take a chance of entering a clinical study such as Dr. Moritz is proposing. I have some hope that his rational hypothesis and method will be successful and useful in clinical practice."

"I am fully aware that Dr. Moritz's study might fail. Or it might only help a certain percent of those patients entered. I might be one of those that do not benefit from the Nanosphere Complex treatment. Even if that is so, when I pass from the living world, I will have had the satisfaction of at least trying the option of entering Dr. Moritz's study."

"Dr. Moritz's research has been honest and factual. I believe he is a moral teacher, clinician, and scientist who wants to do the best as possible for his patients. His work and achievements will, at some time, be recognized for their value. This will be so even after myself and this Committee are no longer part of the picture. I humbly urge the Committee to approve this clinical study protocol so that Dr. Moritz might begin to enter patients as soon as possible. Some of those patients that are hanging on, myself included, do not have much time to wait for many other options."

"Thank you very much Dr. Green, for allowing me to visit your Committee meeting and present my feelings."

The majority of the Committee thanked Jim for coming and speaking his opinions. However, Dr. Green only managed a nod towards Jim, while looking at this watch. It appeared there would be no questions for Jim from the Committee. Dr. Moritz shook Jim's hand and Rita gave Jim a kiss on the forehead. Moritz and Rita then assisted Jim in his wheelchair back out into the hallway. Moritz was assured by Jim that Rita could get him back to their van and that they would be going straight home. Moritz expressed his thanks again to both Jim and Rita for coming to support his study. He then returned to the Committee room and prepared for the next part of the meeting.

* * *

After Moritz returned to the room, Dr. Green said: "Now, to get back to the Committee's business. The plan today is to give the Committee members a final chance to ask Dr. Moritz any further questions about his study. We will then allow Dr. Moritz to present a final statement, as he indicated he would like to do."

"Finally, we will have a vote on Moritz's proposed clinical study. All of those present here, except Dr. Moritz, are eligible to vote. There will be no abstaining votes allowed. In order for the proposal to pass, there must be a majority. Short of a majority or in the case of a tie vote, the study has failed getting approval from this Committee. In that case, the clinical study protocol cannot be initiated at our Lake View Hospital at this time, despite it having received approval from the FDA and the National Cancer Institute. If disapproved here, Dr. Moritz's study protocol cannot be reconsidered at Lake View until 12 months from today, if he should decide to resubmit his protocol request. Are these comments clear to everyone? If not, speak up."

None of the group appeared to have a question on Dr. Green's comments, so he continued: "Then we will open the floor to Committee members for questions of Dr. Moritz if there are any."

Mike Jones raised his hand and spoke: "Dr. Moritz, you know now that there will be an increase in the percent of your grant funds that will be removed and allocated to the Financial Administration of Lake View. Some of this increased percent is going to the Faculty Equity Committee, and other new Committees being formed. This is part of our Administration and Finance Division's effort in working toward a more even compensation for researchers and clinicians at our institution. With these increased dollars removed from your grants, do you still have enough funds to start and complete the clinical study you have proposed?"

Moritz stood and responded: "Mike, thank you for this question. This morning Dr. Chen and I reviewed our research fund situation in detail, factoring in the newly awarded ICCPF grant and your increased withdrawal percentage. We will have to sacrifice a few basic science experiments, planned for the Breast Cancer bone metastases project, but we are on solid financial footing for the next 5 years. In addition, I already have favorable critiques back from other private charitable foundations interested in contributing to our research program. So, through these and our present grants, we will have ample money to fund our basic laboratory research progress, the clinical study through full enrollment, and the three year follow-up of patient outcomes

"Yes, I will certainly feel the loss of the additional money the Administration and Financial Divisions are taking from my awards. Yes, I will continue to disagree with some of the rationale and use of that extra "taxation money."

Moritz showed a partial smile, but had serious eye contact with Mike Jones. He added: "Mike, don't let my fiscal situation keep you from voting 'yes' for this clinical study. I have it covered."

Dr. Lopez was next to address Moritz: "Victor, I will ask it straight out. Can you be totally unbiased and objective during your study? Is there any question in your mind that in some way you might influence the care or outcome of a patient? You are obviously very close to Jim, for example. Can you step back and not control, let's say, entry criteria or the Nanosphere Complex dose for him? Or influence cares that Jim receives during the study? Would you possibly do extra for him because he is your patient? How are you going to handle these issues?"

Moritz said: "Rebecca, I am glad you are bringing this important issue forward. It is likely that other members of the Committee might have the same question."

"You are certainly right that I want the best for Jim. However, I have worked hard on my study protocol to keep it as objective as possible. There are entry criteria that are specific. The dose groups will be assigned randomly by code and not be identified until the study is over after the 3 years follow-up. Unless there are data to indicate dose complications, patients will not be switched from one dose to another, regardless of the course of their condition during the study."

"As the Principle Investigator of the protocol for this clinical study, I cannot and will not be involved with entry or treating any of the patients during the time of their Nanosphere Complex study. The monthly Oncology Physicians rotating through the ward and clinic will be in charge of cares for study patients if they need Hospital admission. There are many other specific details written in the protocol guidelines for ongoing care and outcome assessments."

"Data will be analyzed by a neutral group of oncologists, statisticians, and lay persons under the direction and oversight of the National Institutes of Health and American Cancer Society. So, I believe that the many checks and balances in the study assures that any bias I might have will not affect the assessment, care, or outcome of any patient in the protocol."

"For those of you that know me. You realize that I have tried to demonstrate, in my professional and private life, an objective and moral character in what I do. I hope my history here at Lake View and my words have answered your question."

"Thank you Victor." Dr. Lopez said.

Dr. Green asked: "Are there any more questions for Dr. Moritz at this time? Hearing none, I will ask Dr. Moritz to make his final presentation, after which the vote on the study protocol will proceed."

"Before Dr. Moritz takes the floor, let me speak to the voting again. The voting will consist of each member receiving a 3x5 inch ballot with your individual name typed on it. The ballot will also state the title of Dr. Moritz's clinical study protocol. You will check the 'yes' or 'no' box and sign your ballot above your typed name. You will return the ballots to me for counting and I will share the results with you immediately."

"Now go ahead with your comments, Dr. Moritz."

***

Dr. Victor Moritz looked at his notes again briefly, then stood and spoke: "I want to thank all the Committee members for the time they have spent reviewing my protocol, the time spent in our meetings, and our critique interactions. I obviously believe strongly in my proposal and would appreciate a passing vote, but it is up to you."

"I do not have any more scientific or financial information to present in this time I have to speak today. However, I do have some information to share with the Committee, and it is not pretty."

A few members of the Committee looked around the room at one another and shifted in their chairs.

"First, on the morning of this Committee's initial meeting to review my protocol, two members of the Committee visited my research laboratory fairly early, before I was around. After arriving, they talked with Dr. Li Chen. Dr. Chen is the Post-Doctoral Fellow who has worked extensively with me on our Nanosphere Complex research. To make a fairly long story short, these Committee members were rude and intimidating toward Dr. Chen. They asked her to say that there were research failures in our data that we were hiding, so our proposal of a clinical study would not be compromised. They tried to distort her answers and confuse her with their multiple questions. They even tried to bribe her. They offered to move forward her next scheduled promotion, or a financial bonus if she would make written statements that we were altering experimental findings."

"When I arrived at the lab later that morning, Dr. Chen told me what had happened. She was distraught, obviously shaking and tearful. At the time, I consoled her and promised that I would re-visit this issue at a later time, one of which is now."

"Secondly, this past Tuesday night, one of those two that had visited my lab initially, sitting here at the table with us, entered my lab at 11:25 PM when no one else was there. They opened and read parts of one of our research data notebooks. This was what we call our 'Red Star Notebook', which contains the research data on our recent findings regarding breast cancer metastases to bone. This intruder found certain pages of special interest, and so proceeded to take pictures of those lab book pages with his cell phone camera. Then he left the lab about 45 minutes after his entry."

After a pause to let the points sink in, Moritz continued: "I imagine most of you here cannot believe this unethical action. However, I have what I just told you, on a video recording. That video documents, including the person's identity, what I just described to you. The video was taken by an inconspicuously placed Trail Camera that certainly the visitor was unaware of."

"I was not sure of what actions I should take after these episodes. Should I report this to higher Administrative offices? What consequences might I even expect? It makes me wonder. Do other Committees set up at Lake View also have disrupters or spies on them as well? In any event, I wanted this Committee to know of these breeches of conduct before their vote here today."

"That's the end of what I have to say now, Dr. Green. I will not, at this time, answer any questions on these two items I just presented. Thanks again for the time I was granted."

Moritz sat down and gathered up his notes and placed them into his folder. The room was otherwise very quiet. The Committee members were looking around at each other, wondering what was coming next. Dr. Green stared towards Jerry Smith briefly, then he glanced at each person around the room. Finally, he turned his attention back to the ballots that he held in his hand. Jerry Smith had appeared very uncomfortable in his chair, mostly looking down toward the floor.

After a minute or so, Dr. Green said: "I will now hand out the voting ballots. Don't forget to sign your name after you vote. Dr. Moritz, I would appreciate your leaving the room while we are voting on your proposal."

Moritz left the room and closed the door behind him.

***

It took only a minute or two for the Committee members to mark and sign their ballots. Dr. Green gathered the 6 ballots, counted them at his chair in plain sight of all at the table.

Dr. Green finally said: "It was 3 votes yes, 3 votes no. The protocol has failed to obtain this Committee's approval. Mike, you are sitting nearest to the door. Please go and invite Dr. Moritz back into the room to join us."

When Moritz was back in his seat, Dr. Green spoke: "Dr. Moritz, the vote was a tie at 3 yes, 3 no. As you understand, that means that the Committee did not approve your clinical study protocol. I think we are now finished here."

Victor Moritz quickly responded: "Dr. Green, this Committee might be finished for today, but I will fight your results. I have just told the Committee of two instances of unethical and improper intrusions into my research laboratory by members of this Committee. I cannot believe that the Director of Science or President of Lake View will allow the votes by those two individuals to be valid. That is as a minimum. Further, the Faculty person that was video recorded in the act of copying data from my lab notebook in the middle of the night should face additional reprimands. I have already taken these issues to the Director of Science. He is planning on consulting with the President on further actions to take."

***

Dr. Green started to respond, but suddenly the door of the conference room opened. Director Wright and an Assistant from Lake View's President's Office came into the room. Dr. Moritz and all the Committee members were surprised by this new development in an already unusual meeting.

Director Wright told everyone in the room to keep their seats, and then spoke to them: "Dr. Green, listen to me closely. Dr. Moritz has presented me with undeniable hard evidence that one of your Committee members entered his lab alone in the middle of the night. This person attempted to, and actually did, unethically obtain research material from one of Dr. Moritz's laboratory experiment notebooks, clearly without permission or authorization."

"I have spoken with the President and he has granted me certain authority. Immediately, the vote of that person at this Committee Meeting is declared as illegitimate. The remaining 5 ballots will decide the outcome of Dr. Moritz's clinical study protocol application."

"Secondly, the two members of this Committee that interrogated Dr. Li Chen will face a panel of Faculty member peers. That group will review the facts of that interaction, and consider what possible reprimands these two Committee members should receive. So now, Dr. Green, please give me the ballots of this meeting so that I might do a recount of the eligible votes."

Dr. Green reluctantly handed over the six ballots to Director Wright. Wright selected out the ballot of Jerry Smith, tore it in half and put it aside face down on the table. He then recounted the remaining 5 ballots. Director Wright then said: "The vote is 3 to 2, in favor of allowing Dr. Moritz's clinical study protocol to go forward at Lake View. Dr. Moritz will receive confirmation of this by a letter, signed by me, tomorrow. Congratulations Victor Moritz."

"I thank the Committee members for their work and preparation for the meetings they attended. Efforts of such review Committees are very valuable in helping our continued functioning as a valid Scientific Medical Institution. We appreciate it. That said, the work and function of your Committee is now finished and we are adjourned. Dr. Green and Dr. Smith, you will be asked to the President's office sometime next week. The purpose will be to review the verbal and video evidence that Dr. Moritz has provided to me and this Committee today. After that, as I said earlier, a Faculty Committee on disciplinary action will meet and decide if further actions will be taken."

Then Director Wright took the ballots and he and the President's Assistant left the room. Following that, Dr. Green, Dr. Smith, and Mike Jones also left the room, talking together as they walked down the hall towards the elevators.

However, Dr. Rebecca Lopez, Dr. Phil Johnson, and Rob Olson gathered around Victor Moritz, shaking his hand with congratulations and wishing him luck and success with his Nanosphere Complex clinical study.

16

Dr. Victor Moritz left the conference room feeling exhausted, but grateful that his study finally had been approved. He could hardly believe the events that had occurred and he wanted to spread the great news. Also, he realized that he must begin the work on getting the study up and running as soon as possible.

It was late afternoon when Moritz got to the lab to tell Dr. Chen, Mark and Charlie of the approval. After their congratulations, Charlie had to leave for a Medical Students' meeting, and Mark left for a previous commitment with his wife.

Li Chen and Moritz went into their office to talk. Victor told Li about speaking with the Director of Science regarding Green and Smith's uninvited visit to the lab and their questioning her. He told her he reviewed the video material on Jerry Smith for the entire Committee. Finally, he summarized the voting process and the visit at the meeting by Director Wright. Moritz told Dr. Chen of Wright's comments to the Committee and the plans for additional evaluations and reprimands for Dr. Green and Dr. Smith. Li Chen expressed her happiness to Moritz that the clinical study could now go forward.

Moritz asked Dr. Chen to begin preparing

some of each of the three concentration doses of the Nanosphere Complex when she came to work in the morning. This would take a few days, and he wanted the doses available by the time the first patient was ready to be entered into the study. He expected this would take about 2 weeks.

After that, Moritz put a copy of the study protocol into his briefcase and began to leave the office. Before leaving, he told Li Chen how much he appreciated all her dedicated work, which had helped lead to this day. He suggested that she take the rest of the afternoon off, and waved goodbye. Then Moritz went to his vehicle in the parking lot and drove home to the cabin.

***

After changing clothes, Moritz took grain to the steers, fed and exercised Shadow. Then he and Shadow went inside. Victor poured a glass of wine and set out a plate of cheese and shelled walnuts for a snack. He sat down in the kitchen with his phone and dialed the home of Jim and Rita Davis.

Rita answered the phone and Moritz said: "Rita, I have some news for you and Jim. This afternoon, the Committee passed my clinical study. Thank you for getting Jim to the meeting today, by the way. If Jim feels well enough to talk on the phone,

I would like to tell him the good news myself."

Rita said: "That is great news! Thank you so much. Jim is right here. I'll give him the phone."

Jim, speaking with a rather weak voice: "Hello, who is this?"

Moritz said: "Jim, its Victor Moritz. I wanted to tell you that the Committee approved my clinical study protocol. I will be working on getting things in place to start as soon as possible. It should be ready for patient screening and entry in a couple of weeks. I want to thank you and Rita for making the effort to come to the Committee meeting and support the study. I appreciated your comments. How was the rest of your day?"

Jim replied, in a voice that sounded stronger now: "Rita drove us home just fine as usual. I have taken a nap, then swallowed my medications as I ate some dinner. This news helps make my day a better one. Whenever the screening begins for patient entry, I will be applying. Thanks a lot for calling, Dr. Moritz."

Jim and Moritz spoke for a few minutes longer, mostly about non-medical issues, then said their goodbyes. As Jim was giving the phone back to Rita, Moritz overheard Jim say: "Dear Rita, we might have another chance to have some more time together." Then the phone signal went silent.

After a short break to pet Shadow, Moritz dialed the Cardiology ward of Lake View Hospital and asked about Otto. He was told by the ward clerk that Otto was discharged and picked up by his daughter at around two o'clock. Moritz thanked the clerk, and then dialed the home of Otto Zellers.

Zellers' phone was answered by Amy, somewhat surprising Moritz when she picked up.

"Amy, this is Victor Moritz. Remember, I am a friend of your Dad's, and you and I have met a couple of times."

Victor continued: "How are things going for you and your Dad since his discharge this afternoon?"

Amy said: "Things are good and we are adjusting. He was glad to return home."

Victor asked further: "If he is awake and feels up to talking on the phone for a short time, would it be alright with you to put him on?"

Victor heard Otto in the background asking who was on the phone, as Amy was telling Victor to just wait until she took the phone to her Dad.

Hearing Otto on the phone then, Moritz said: "Otto, sorry to call you so soon after you got out of the hospital. Are you feeling well enough to talk for a few minutes?"

Otto spoke rather loudly into the phone: "Hello, Victor, how did the Committee vote go? I am anxious to know. I'll tell you more about myself after you give me the news on your protocol."

Victor, after taking a good swallow of his wine, responded: "Otto, the clinical study protocol passed the Committee, 3 yes, 2 no."

"This approval came only with some difficulty. The Director of Science, Dr. Stan Wright, appeared at the end of the meeting with a representative from the President's office. Director Wright and the President had decided to declare the vote of Jerry Smith invalid. That broke a previous 3 to 3 tie vote. After that, Director Wright, in front of the whole Committee, informed Dr. Green and Jerry that they would be called to a meeting with the President in a few days. Their interaction with Dr. Chen in the lab, and Jerry's invasion of our lab notebook will be reviewed and some punishment will hopefully come out of it."

Otto then interrupted: "Oh Victor, I am so happy to hear this good news that you can proceed with your study. However, don't forget what I said regarding expectations from some Lake View Administrative positions. Don't get your hopes up too high yet. Consider being happy with what you won today, and just get going with your study."

Victor responded: "Otto, thanks for all your support over this. I will also keep in mind your advice and reservations on what else might happen to Green and Smith. Getting this study going forward will keep me so busy that I probably won't be thinking much about their meeting with the President."

"Now Otto, tell me about how you are feeling and how you and Amy are getting settled back at home."

Otto said: "Amy and I left the Hospital earlier this afternoon. They took me from my room to her car in a wheel chair, which I was glad for, since it was quite a distance. Amy had brought a box of candy for me to leave at the Nurse's station, and I thanked all those I saw there for the care they had given me. I will probably write a note to the Cardiology ward so others might know that I was very satisfied with the care I received."

"Amy had shopped for a lot of groceries already so we came directly home. We settled in without any problems. As I rested on the couch, she made us a good meal of chicken breast and cooked vegetables. The sugar cookies were from the store, but they were a good treat. Amy promised to do some baking and more cooking the next couple of days. She will put a lot into the freezer for me. That will cut down on my needing to be in the kitchen for long periods the next few days. I hope to be back to my previous strength soon, but I guess it will take a week or two."

"Amy will stay through the week-end and start back to her home on Monday morning. She was hoping that you could come over sometime this week-end to touch bases with us about when and how often you might be planning on checking in on me. If you are able to do that, just give us a call. So far, I feel pretty good, all things considered. Thank you for calling me after your own eventful day."

Victor said he would be able to see Otto and Amy over the week-end and he would give them a call to set up the time. After that, Otto and Victor said goodbye until they would see each other, and ended their call.

***

As evening approached, Moritz took a break to eat a sandwich, then sat again and dialed Ruth in Phoenix.

Ruth answered, recognizing Victor's number: "Vic, I have been hoping for a call from you. Tell me what's going on, after you tell me you still love and miss me."

Victor's mood was immediately better, and he said: "Oh Ruth. Yes, of course I love you and will until the day I die. I do miss you. It has been a wild day back here. Let me give you a quick summary and then we can get to talking about us. OK with you?"

Ruth replied: "Of course, Vic, it is so great to hear your voice. Tell me all that has been going on"

Victor then reviewed with Ruth the highlights of the day and the Committee meeting. He started with the visit to Director Wright's office, which surprised Ruth, and he told her of Jim's statement to the Committee. Victor described his telling the Committee of the lab visit by Green and Smith, the video tape evidence against Smith, and the first vote. Then Victor told about the appearance of Director Wright and vote recount. Ruth was very happy and congratulatory to Victor about the approval of his study protocol.

After hearing about Otto, she expressed her thankfulness that he was stable and discharged from the hospital.

Victor then said: "Now, what about you, dear Ruth?"

Ruth said: "Well, my days at work and here at the apartment have been pretty routine. Not that exciting, I guess, but certainly fulfilling when a patient improves, or at least is made more comfortable due to our cares."

"As to us, Vic, I talked to my supervisor this week about the possibility of my moving to your neck of the woods. She said she would certainly miss me, but will be happy to write a very good reference and evaluation letter for me to accompany any future job application whenever I might need it. She said that she was certain the Director of Nursing of the Hospital would also write a favorable recommendation. Finally, to my pleasant surprise, she added that more than one Physician that I have worked with on the wards would gladly write a complimentary note as well. So overall, I feel real good about her feedback."

Victor said: "Ruth, this is good news. I expected that you would receive great evaluations. I know of your attitude and commitment to do the best in whatever you undertake. We should start talking about a possible timetable for us. What were you thinking along those lines?"

Ruth paused and then said: "Well, Vic, actually it will take me two months or so to finish here in Phoenix. For one, my boss already has asked if I would help in evaluating persons when they recruit for my position. I agreed to help with that because she has treated me so fairly while I have been here."

"There is also another thing. As you know, last year I initiated a change in several nursing procedures related to our Pediatric Oncology patients. This has been generating data on Nursing outcomes, utilization and satisfaction of patients and their parents' attitudes for the past year. I would like to finish analyzing the data and writing up a report on this project to submit to my supervisor and Director of Nursing. Hopefully, some of the innovations might then be adopted by the Nursing Department and the Hospital. So I think there would be two to three months before I could leave here."

"During that time I would also be making arrangements for shipping some furniture and personal items to your place, cleaning my apartment for moving out, and so forth. Vic, how does that sound to you for starters?"

Victor said: "Ruth, it sounds like you have been giving some serious thought to our situation. I would be happy to fly down and help you with driving your remaining possessions up to my, soon to be, our home. Whatever you decide on my helping or not will be all right with me."

Ruth answered: "Yes, I would like your help with that part of the move for sure."

Victor continued: "Your suggested time line fits

well with me for a couple reasons. For sure, just a few more months is a lot better than, for example, a year, before we are together."

"For me, the next few weeks will be very busy, like yours. I am committed to look in on Otto several times a week until he feels up to his usual routine activities. Additionally, it will take me a few weeks to get the study started and enrolling patients. Our lab will be busy synthesizing more of the Nanosphere-Complex so that the appropriate doses are available for patients."

"We have several patients identified as interested in entering the study. They still need to be screened and interviewed. There will be permission papers to be signed, lab data and other forms that need final preparation for use. I must be sure all this is being done properly. I will also be working with Lake View Hospital to finalize arrangements for use of the outpatient clinical space. The Research Nurses must be orientated for the infusions of the Nanospheres, and observation care until the patient leaves the Hospital clinic.

"The first patients entered will be from our own clinic patient pool. Then we will complete setting up mechanisms that extend information and seek patients to enter the study from locations that are further out in our region."

"So Ruth, it will take a while at this end for me to have things running smoothly with the clinical study and in the lab. We will just have to keep in touch often during the next few weeks about our progress, and make new or alter plans as needed."

"Ruth, you know that I would love it if you were able to come up to live with me starting tomorrow. But, we both will be happier, I believe, if we work hard on our projects now and look forward to getting together as soon as we can after that. Okay with you?"

Ruth answered: "Yes, Vic, I agree with you. I have my things to do and you have lots of work getting the study going. I will still love you whenever we finally do get together. I hope you realize that."

Victor and Ruth finished their phone conversation, both feeling good about their communication and tentative plans.

***

The next morning, Dr. Moritz went to his laboratory and outlined a schedule for the day. Dr. Chen arrived at 7:00 AM and they reviewed plans for the timing and amounts of Nanosphere Complex needed to get started when the first patients were enrolled into the study.

Moritz then arranged a meeting to occur next Monday morning. That meeting included the outpatient clinic manager, the clinic Nursing supervisor, and appropriate representatives of radiology imagining and clinical laboratory services. He notified the Hospital's Research Protocol Office to contact the two Research Nurse specialists that he had arranged to hire to help oversee several aspects of the study. Some of their functions would be contacting prospective patients that might qualify for the study. After the patient was given the details of the study and informed consent was agreed, the patient would be, randomly and by coded identity, assigned to a Nanosphere Complex dose level. The patient would be contacted for an entry medical evaluation and a schedule arranged for their first dose. Then they would actually proceed through the protocol.

Late in the afternoon, Moritz went to the Public Relations office of Lake View and worked on a letter that would be sent to clinics and Physicians in the local area and further out into the region around Lake View. This letter contained an announcement about the beginning of the clinical study of the Nanosphere Complex treatment of patients with prostate cancer that had then metastasized to bone. The mailing would include a brief explanation of the study, patient eligibility, how the expenses would be paid, and contact numbers for those interested or needing other information.

***

Two weeks after Moritz's study was approved at Lake View, two patients were admitted to the outpatient research clinic. One was Jim Davis. Baseline lab and imaging studies were first. After these, entry and dose randomization occurred and then the study patients received their first infusion of the Nanosphere Complex. No apparent side effects with the infusions were seen. Therefore, the patients were discharged the same day, as planned in the study protocol. They were given written and verbal reminders about follow-up studies, and their next appointments in 3 weeks and 6 weeks for the remaining infusions.

Moritz, as Principal Investigator for the study, visited briefly with each patient to get acquainted. However, he was not involved in patient entry, randomization of dose, cares, or evaluations of patient progress. He was completely unaware of the dose of any specific patient or of their blood chemistry and radiation imaging results.

For example, he knew Jim Davis had entered

the study. However, each patient was given a code identity so that all assessments were only identified by that code. All identity codes were being kept confidential under lock and key until all study results had been submitted to and reviewed by the oversight panel at the NIH.

***

About six weeks after starting the clinical study, Moritz received a call from Dr. Phil Johnson. He asked if Moritz could meet him sometime soon for a chat about certain issues developing at Lake View. He also wanted to talk with Moritz about a personal item that had come up recently. They had made arrangements for Moritz to go to Johnson's office today, which was a couple of days after that call.

When finished reviewing some minor issues with Dr. Chen in the lab this morning, Moritz started for Johnson's office. Dr. Johnson's office door was open and he saw Moritz coming. He got up from his desk, welcomed Moritz with a handshake and motioned towards a chair for Moritz while he sat back down at his desk.

Johnson said: "Victor, thank you for coming today. I have two or three things on my mind I want to talk with you about. First, please tell me how your clinical study is going. I am so glad we, the Committee, finally got it approved so you could get started."

Moritz replied: "Phil, thanks again for your help while on the Committee."

"The trial so far has five patients enrolled. The first ones entered have already received their second dose of Nanosphere Complex. Three other patients will soon get the second blood and imaging studies to follow size, distribution of bone metastases and if there are any effects on blood chemistry values. Then they will receive their second dose.

"The NIH panel will not start reviewing outcome data until laboratory and imaging data are completed after their third and final dose. Then the study will assess patients with the scheduled assessments at 6 months, at 1 year, and 3 years after entry. All the follow up data is being sent to the NIH review panel. Their review will continue to be done under coded conditions, so no bias or patient identification can be introduced into the analysis."

"I am happy to say, Phil, that so far we have not seen any obvious negative side effects of the therapy when the patients have been in the Clinic for their Nanosphere Complex infusions. I am obviously keeping my fingers crossed."

Johnson said: "That is good news, Victor. I hope things keep going well for your study."

Johnson, his expression more serious, continued: "Victor, I don't know how much you are aware of some of the developments and ideas that several of the Administrative sections are undertaking here at Lake View."

Victor said: "To be perfectly honest Phil, I have not heard much since those things at the Committee meeting about the Faculty Equity efforts and taking more money from funded research grants. I did also hear that Jerry Smith was removed from the Oncology Department, but I don't know if he got hired at some other place. I haven't heard about Dr. Green. What new developments are you talking about?"

Johnson said: "Well, Victor, Dr. David Green is very close to the President of Lake View and has many supporters. So, he barely got his wrists slapped for the morning he and Jerry went to your lab and talked with Dr. Chen. It came down to his description of the interaction versus how Dr. Chen perceived the encounter. Green got off with essentially not even a noticeable reprimand."

"Green also claimed he had no part in Jerry Smith's entry into your lab and filming lab book pages. This was suspicious to some of the Faculty because Jerry claimed that Green had suggested, or at least knew of and condoned, Jerry's actions. Green denied it."

"Finally, he received no criticism from the President about how he ran our Committee's meetings. I, Rebecca and Rob Olson had even written a letter to the President and Science Director Wright. We wrote about things like unilaterally bringing in Mike Jones with the new rules on claiming more grant money for "Indirect Costs", and giving Mike voting privileges. Some of us on the Committee also thought David Green had a condescending attitude towards Rob Olson and Jim Davis. Maybe we were being too subjective with that opinion. Anyway, David Green is still going strong."

"Victor, I want to alert you of something Green is up to. He is trying to push through Administration a rule that protocols, like your bone metastases study, be reviewed, in full detail, yearly by Committees before any can continue to enroll patients. This is his attempt, though disguised, to strike back at you so he can settle the score. But setting that aside, this rule is bad for any study, present and in the future. Imagine, if a yearly Committee decided against a study that was already in progress. What a waste of time and research funds! Think of that effect on patients that had already enrolled, and their pain and anxiety. Their entry into a study might now be discontinued by Committee action. I can agree with a yearly progress report being required for a Committee review. Yes, also Committee review if there were obvious negative effects on patients, but I think a full Committee review of an established study, again in detail as the first evaluation, is going a little too far."

Moritz said nothing to all this information. He sat there looking at Phil Johnson, shaking his head slowly with an astonished look on his face.

Phil Johnson continued: "Victor, let me briefly tell you what else is happening here at Lake View from the top down. There are more Faculty Equity adjustments and regulations, some from Green's Committee. Others are just handed down by the President and the Financial Department."

"Within a few months, I hear, there will be several more changes. All medical Faculty in a particular Division, let's say Oncology, will be on an equal salary after their first two years in the Department. It will be regardless of the Clinician's years in practice or level of expertise. This will be even if a Physician decides or desires to work more than the regulated 40 hours per week. So, no adjusted salary for more effort."

"Also, patients will be assigned to Physicians in the Department according to who is next on the list for a patient. This is designed to keep the patient load equal for all Clinicians. The patient will not have a choice to see the Physician they already know, and has already cared for them. This assignment will occur regardless, even if a patient feels a certain Physician in the system has demonstrated a higher level of expertise above others in the Department's Physician pool. So, patients will be assigned to equalize the patient/physician ratio. This is planned instead of allowing the patient to choose the Physician they prefer, and Physicians now cannot control their own number of patients."

"Finally, Lake View Hospital will determine the fee for a Physician's procedure and cares. This will be a uniform charge, regardless of the Physician performing the service. In my opinion, this fee regulation punishes the Physician that might have gained, through their own efforts, special expertise in a procedure or care approach. It also discourages some intangibles. For example, no credit is given to a Physician for extra time spent talking with the patient or making other extra efforts to facilitate a better Physician-patient relationship or better understanding of the patient-family dynamics occurring. To top it off, Valley View's Administrative and Financial Departments will keep a higher percent of these new regulated and dictated fees for the Physicians' work with patients. These changes are coming Victor, and I wanted you to be aware of them."

***

Johnson went on before Victor could ask any questions.

"Victor, another topic I wanted to share with you. I have accepted a job as Director of Science and Translational Medicine at a newly established 'Rocky Peaks Cancer Program'. This Program is being administered independently, but is closely affiliated with the University of Colorado Medical School in Aurora. Rocky Peaks is located a few miles Northwest of Denver, at the eastern side of the Rocky Mountains. As such, the weather is tolerable, to say the least. There are lots of days of sunshine and great opportunities for outdoor activities. Much of the large metropolitan population between Denver and Boulder will have easy access to this new Cancer Program. The Program will offer comprehensive cancer care, including of course, diagnosis, established and state of the art treatment, basic and translational research, education, you name it. I think it will be a very successful facility."

"My lab, and my family of course, are preparing to leave Lake View in four weeks. I am now working on hiring Oncology Physicians and Scientists for the part of the Program that I am responsible for."

"Victor, I would really like for you to join the group I am putting together. Consider this conversation as a job offer, and please give it serious consideration. You would be able to move all your awarded extramural grants along with you. We will guarantee you as much lab space as you have now and maybe more. Dr. Chen and your graduate student, Mark, would be welcome to come with you. Most of the supplies and equipment you use here at Lake View that was purchased with your grant money can be moved as well. If there is any equipment you might need, but Lake View won't allow you to remove, my budget at Rocky Peaks will supply the items for you there."

"You would be allowed to schedule and care for as many clinic patients that you feel you have time for. We expect that you will realize when your clinic schedule is full and needs limits. This can be adjusted if you decide to spend more or less time in your laboratory. We would also expect you to spend around 20 percent of your time doing the excellent teaching I know you do. I can guarantee your salary, laboratory facilities, and peer support will be much better than here at Lake View. Victor, please give this offer some thought."

"Victor said: "Phil, I already am giving it some positive thought and consideration. An issue for me, obviously, is what would happen with my clinical study with the Nanosphere Complex? Would I be able to continue that work at Rocky Peaks?"

Phil, now even more enthused, replied: "Victor, you certainly can continue your study at that facility, after you pass the appropriate protocol review channels. I guarantee that you will pass that test. In addition, it is important for you to know that the area's population around our site is much larger than here around Lake View, so your enrollment goals could be reached sooner."

"Regarding your already enrolled patients here at Lake View, consider this. You could keep some finances here at Lake View to complete the study doses and evaluations on the five patients that you have entered already. You would then begin the same protocol in Colorado. The NIH review committee will likely be uncomfortable reviewing and combining the outcome data from the two different sites. If so, you could just restart patient entry at Rocky Peaks and use the data of the patients from our Cancer Program. NIH reviewers would agree with that."

"If that were the case, then you might be able to use any data you obtained on the five patients at Lake View as a preliminary report for the NIH, as your new study went forward in Colorado."

"Victor said: "Phil, thanks for all this information you gave to me about Lake View. I also am a little overwhelmed, but really appreciate the job offer in Colorado. I will talk to Ruth about this and try to consider everything. How long does your offer stand for me?"

"Dr. Johnson said: "Victor, take eight weeks to think about it. If you have any other questions about the offer, ask me whatever, or whenever, you like."

As Moritz left his office, Johnson was satisfied that Victor would be a great fit on the Faculty at the Rocky Peaks Cancer Program.

17

The week he talked with Dr. Phil Johnson had been very busy for Moritz. Today, after finishing his work at the office, Moritz left in the late afternoon to drop by Otto Zeller's place. Amy had returned to her home and family. Since then, Victor had continued checking if Otto needed to be driven anywhere or if there were other tasks that he might need help with.

Otto generally was doing well on his own since coming home from   the Hospital. He had gained physical strength back to the level before his arrhythmia. He was also having increased confidence about caring for himself, taking medications, and re-establishing communication with some of his other buddies around the area. Victor usually dropped in to visit Otto a couple times a week.

Arriving at Otto's home, Victor checked the mailbox and also brought the daily newspaper from the driveway up to the house. Otto had the door already unlocked and yelled for Victor to come on in. He had just finished his early evening meal of soup, sandwich, and tea.

Otto and Victor greeted each other and settled down in Otto's study to talk. Otto thanked Victor for bringing in the mail and paper. He told Victor that he had a good day and couldn't think of anything that Victor needed to do for him this evening. Maybe in three or four days, he would need to be driven to the Supermarket again to stock up on some food staples. Victor said he would be happy to help and for Otto to just give him a call and they would work it out. Victor suggested that maybe they might even have a light meal at a local restaurant before grocery shopping that day. Otto thought that was a good idea.

The two friends talked a little about the weather, and the last time Victor had spoken with Ruth on the phone. Victor asked Otto about Amy and family and if she was keeping in touch with him. Otto said she calls him twice a week and he tells her how he is feeling and getting along. She still wants him to move closer to her family, but he was not deciding on that yet.

A while later, Otto shifted the conversation by saying: "OK Victor, tell me about your clinical study and how the research is going in your lab?"

Victor responded: "Well, Otto, the lab is busy. We are keeping our basic research projects going, but at a little slower pace than usual. Dr. Chen has to spend some of her time being sure we have enough Nanosphere Complex medication ready for the needs of the patients we enroll in the study. As you know, each patient entry will receive three infusions of the particular dose they have been randomly assigned."

"As usual though, Dr. Chen is on top of all our projects. Mark is at the stage in his training where he is now more independent in his research. Therefore, Li doesn't need to spend much time looking into what he is doing. He is also now writing his Dissertation and a manuscript for publication on the results of his work. He will be awarded a PhD. at the end of this semester."

"Regarding the progress of the clinical study, I have a concern. Thus far, it is yet unproven suspicions, but I want to share with you what might be happening."

Otto interrupted: "Oh no, Victor! Are they now trying to discredit you and your study?"

Victor began: "Well Otto, as you know, we are now over six weeks and five patients into the study. The clinic registration is going well.   The intravenous infusions of the Nanosphere Complex preparation has no problems.   None of the five patients have had any apparent side effects while they were receiving the material. The Nursing staff in the clinic have been great and they are working well with the Research Nurses in understanding and using protocol guidelines. We have good cooperation with the imaging procedures and lab blood drawing requirements being conducted when they are scheduled and needed. So, most things are clicking very well."

Otto said: "Yes, it sounds like your study has gotten off to a good start. But Victor, it seems you also have some bad news lurking that you are concerned about."

***

Victor took a break and walked around Otto's study for a minute. He then sat back down and continued: "Otto, I have heard a rumor that the code that hides the patients' identity from their dose of Nanosphere Complex has been broken. If so, there is not a blinded evaluation of each patient and dose. Thus, the study can be potentially biased, and this means we cannot honestly use the follow- up data we are gathering on these five patients."

"Here is what I know so far, which has all happened in the last 24 hours. As you know, I try to visit briefly with each patient on the day they are in the clinic to receive their infusion of their coded Nanosphere Complex dose. When talking with a patient yesterday afternoon, he told me he overheard a conversation between the two clinic doctors that are caring for the study patients.   He said it was something about how the code of patient's identity and dose had gotten leaked out to some person in the Hospital. This patient talking with me knew nothing else, and seemed not to be concerned. I did not ask him any more questions about it."

Otto, shaking his head, said: "Victor, this is terrible!"

Victor continued: "So, Otto, I had planned to talk to those two Physicians this morning. Before I did so, they appeared at my lab as I was heading for the door to locate them. They were straight forward with me, and very apologetic."

"They had learned of this code leak yesterday morning. By chance, they had overheard a Hospital's Research Data Administrative Assistant talking on the phone. She was giving the five names of the study patients and their Nanosphere dose code information to someone. They assumed it was a Physician, since she addressed the person on the phone as Doctor, but no last name."

"Then later in the morning, a patient apparently had over- heard these Physicians discussing it between themselves at the infusion area of the clinic. That was the patient that in the afternoon told me of hearing about it."

"I thanked these two Physicians for coming and telling me of this unexpected and unethical breech in the study's protocol. I told them, frankly, that they should have contacted me immediately and should have been more discreet when talking between themselves in public and especially among patients. I let them know that they have already been heard talking about this by at least one patient, and made it clear that they were not to discuss this further with anyone else, not even between themselves."

"We discussed briefly about what to do next. I told them to just keep focused on their work in the clinic for now. This was my problem and I would be deciding how to pursue it. Fortunately, no new patients were scheduled to enter the study and none were returning for the second or third Nanosphere infusion the rest of the week. They left my lab saying they were very sorry about this breech of study data and their blunder of being overheard discussing it."

"That was this morning. I then scheduled a meeting with the Hospital's Research Data Administrative Assistant for the first thing tomorrow morning. I also made an appointment for tomorrow with Science Director Wright."

"Otto, can you believe it? Obviously, I have

been spending a lot of time thinking about this, and of course losing some sleep last night over it as well."

Otto said: "Victor, I am so sorry for this problem. I'll tell you right now that I think Dr. Green, and maybe the President himself, are involved with this breech of confidentially in your clinical study. It is certainly not ethical behavior by those involved."

Victor said: "Yes, Otto, it all is unbelievable to me at this time as well. Tomorrow I will start probing and making some decisions, and I have that meeting scheduled with Science Director Wright. Now, I also want to tell you about some information that Phil Johnson told me recently."

Otto interrupted: "Victor, before you start, I need to take a break and go to the bathroom. How about you getting a couple of beers out of the refrigerator, and I'll be back shortly."

Victor said: "Good idea my friend. I will do that."

After the break, and each with a beer had returned to the study, Victor began: "Well, Phil Johnson wanted to talk to me and I was with him for an hour or so last week in his office. He told me about some changes coming that affects the Medical Faculty at Lake View. Briefly, for one, all Physicians in each Division will be on equal salaries after their first two years, regardless of skill level, seniority, or other factors."

"Secondly, patients are going to be assigned to Physicians on a rotating basis. This will be regardless of the patient's Physician preference or a Physician's experience and expertise".

"Third, Lake View is determining fee charges, which will be the same for all the Physicians in a particular Division, irrespective of any different levels of effort or competency of individual Physicians. The Administration will keep a higher percent of these now equal fees."

Otto interrupted again: "Victor, it's like I told you a few weeks ago. The Lake View present administration is trying to discourage their Medical Staff and Researchers from becoming competitive, independent and productive members of their profession. These plans you just told me will lead to Administrative elites denying individual rights of the Faculty, as your information from Johnson confirms."

"A Faculty's individual property, which is one's drive to excellence and expertise in their particular practice of medicine or research, is being taken from them. Your individual property rights are being reduced to making a collective group of workers, controlled by the Administrators at the top that make the changes. To me, this defines, at least, the beginnings of Socialism at the level of the Lake View Medical Center. Is this happening in other medical facilities in our region?"

Victor, after listening closely to Otto, said: "Otto, I think you are right with what you are saying, and it sounds like this trend is getting a firm foothold at Lake View. I don't know about other Medical Programs around our area."

"Now let me take a few more minutes and tell you what else Phil Johnson had to say. He is about to embark on a new job."

Moritz went on to tell Otto about Johnson leaving Lake View to become Director of Science and Translational Medicine at the Rocky Peaks Cancer Program. He reviewed with Otto that Johnson had offered him a position in the Oncology Division that included adequate laboratory space and support for his research program. He said that Johnson had pointed out several advantages of a position at Rocky Peaks, compared to what was developing at Lake View.

Victor said: "Otto, all things considered over the last several weeks here at Lake View, I am going to think seriously about this job offer. Of course, Ruth will have to be in agreement."

Otto said, without hesitation, that Victor should definitely consider this offer and wished him the best of luck should he take it. Noting the time at nearly seven thirty in the evening, Victor and Otto agreed it was getting relatively late. They said goodnight, promising to keep in touch.

***

Moritz's drive to his cabin went quickly, while his mind kept reviewing the day's events. This kept him wide awake and focused on the road.

After the evening routine with the animals, and a bite to eat, Moritz settled in the living room with Shadow on his rug by the door. After starting a small fire in the fireplace stove to take the chill off the room, Moritz picked up the phone as he got comfortable by the fireplace, and called Ruth.

Moritz told Ruth of the last couple days in essentially the same detail as he had Otto. She was astonished and disappointed in the apparent undermining of Victor's clinical study. She hardly knew what to say to support him in this latest assault on his attempt to achieve an answer to the possible Nanosphere Complex effects on bone metastases.

They lingered talking about the patient code breaking problem for a few more minutes.   Victor then started telling Ruth about going to Phil Johnson's office, which he had not previously shared with her. He gave her a summary of the Administrative changes underway regarding the financial and patient distribution plan at Lake View. Before he had finished, Ruth asked him to stop with all the negatives.

Ruth said: "Vic, I doubt that there is anything you can do about this situation. It must be so frustrating for you to watch this happening. Are any other Faculty, or even some of the Administrative hierarchy, as troubled by this as you are?"

Victor welcomed the opportunity now to tell Ruth about Phil Johnson's plans and offer. Victor said: "Well Ruth, as a matter of fact, I think there are several Faculty that are against these developments at Lake View."

"As I said, Phil told me about the changes coming. In addition, he told me that he was offered, and has accepted, the position of Director of Science and Translational Medicine at a new cancer institute in Colorado. It is called the 'Rocky Peaks Cancer Program'. He gave Lake View notice, and is leaving next month to start at his new position."

"Ruth, he offered me an appointment there as an adult Oncology Physician and Research Scientist. He promised lab space and strong support for my research. There would be Program money for myself, Li Chen and Mark. I also would be able to transfer most of my already awarded research grant funds to that site without any problems."

"Rocky Peaks is an independent program, but is closely affiliated with the University of Colorado Medical School's education, clinical and research programs in Aurora. Phil said the location of the program, Northwest of Denver, has a fairly large and growing population. So, the location would offer a good setting for clinical studies, such as the protocol that we just started here and now has been sabotaged."

"Ruth, what is your opinion of this offer? Should we think about making this move?"

Ruth said, happily shouting into her phone: "Oh Vic, I think it is a great time for you to leave Lake View, and the opportunity has presented itself! If you are asking me, I would certainly love to go there. I would be with you as we have been planning. I already told you that I have started winding down things here in Phoenix. So, Yes, my love, Yes!"

Victor and Ruth talked for another half hour and then said goodnight to each other. Victor was excited about the possibility of joining Johnson's program in Colorado. Along with that, he was very disturbed about the things he had heard from Johnson, and the terrible clinical study coding breech happening the last two days.

In spite of these tensions, Victor switched to thinking about being with Ruth in the near future. With that, he was able to relax and go to sleep for a much needed rest. Tomorrow was going to be a busy day.

***

Moritz again arrived early at his lab the following morning. He worked through what he was going to say to the five patients now enrolled in the study. The code identifying which patient had received which concentration of Nanosphere Complex had been broken. This could potentially enter bias and thus it now invalidates the use of their follow-up, outcome data, and conclusions.

When Dr. Chen and Mark arrived, he talked to each briefly about their current experiments, but said nothing about yesterday or what he was about to do today.

At 8:30 AM, Dr. Victor Moritz entered the Hospital's Research Data Center's office. He located the person handling his Nanosphere study, whose name was Norma. She and most of the research data section employees were part of the

President's Administrative Assistant pool.

Norma asked Dr. Moritz to have a seat as he entered her cubicle area, which was in a large open room with at least twelve to fifteen other staffed cubicles. Moritz said thanks, but he would stand. Then speaking: "Norma, I will get straight to the point. Did you break the patient dosing code of my Nanosphere Complex study, and reveal it to another person over the phone? I have two witnesses that say they overheard you doing so. I need for you to tell me the name of the person you were phoning this information to, and why you were doing it."

Norma became visibly flushed, glanced around at the room and then held her eyes to the floor. She said she remembered the scene two days ago. Two Physicians were in the area near her cubicle when she was making the call Moritz was asking about. It must have been those two that had overheard her conversation.

Norma decided between lying to Moritz versus admitting her action. She said: "Dr. Moritz, I did what I was told to do by my boss. I relayed the patients' names and codes for the dose they had been assigned in the study to another person. To be honest, it was that or lose my job. I am not proud of my action, but that was the option I had. I have recently become a single mom and I sorely need my employment at Lake View. That being understood, you will realize that I cannot tell you the person I was talking to about your study."

By this time, Norma was starting to cry and others in the office pool were looking towards Moritz and Norma's location. Since Moritz already knew that she was addressing a Doctor on the phone with this information, Moritz decided to drop any further questioning. He told Norma she should consider exposing any future illegitimate activities at Lake View as soon as she knows about them. He thanked her for talking with him, then left Norma's cubicle and the room.

***

Since he had no clinic patients scheduled today, Moritz went to his clinic office to think about what he wanted to cover with Director Wright in the afternoon. He also organized some thoughts about what he now had to do to salvage and to accomplish the goals of his medical career and his research program. After that, he grabbed a quick lunch, then he went to Director Wright's office.

Director Wright welcomed Moritz into his office, offered a chair for him, and while returning to his desk, said: "Victor, tell me how your clinical study is going, and what can I do for you today?"

Victor took a seat in a chair beside the Director's desk. He then told Director Wright about the past two days of his unimaginable disappointment regarding the breaking of the patients' Nanosphere Complex dose code. Victor reviewed how he found out about it and then the confirmation told to him by Norma just this morning.

Although Director Wright wanted to stop Moritz and discuss the study problem issue, Moritz continued, saying he wanted to share something else first. He then told Director Wright about his visit to Phil Johnson's office. Wright nodded his head and said he knew of Johnson's acceptance of the offer at Rocky Peaks Cancer Program. He agreed that was a great position for Phil and had encouraged him to take the job.

Wright also had heard of the new administrative decisions on physician salaries, patient distribution, and charged fees that was making its way through most Departments at Lake View. He agreed with Victor that these initiatives would turn out to be bad ideas for the entire Lake View Medical Center. Wright admitted his frustration that he had little influence on these decisions coming down from upper Administrative and financial channels.

After those comments, Director Wright said: "Now Victor, tell me what you are thinking about this whole picture. First, the breech of the patient dose code, so their data cannot be used as valid for your study. Secondly, what about all the changes at Lake View, and how about Phil Johnson's decision?"

Victor moved toward the edge of his chair, facing Stan Wright, and said: "Director Wright, I want to tell you how much I respect you and the way you carry out your responsibilities. I also especially thank you so very much for your help in getting my Nanosphere protocol Committee approval."

"I will miss you and your council very much. After thinking all things over several times, I have decided to leave Lake View within a few weeks. I will join Phil Johnson's program at Rocky Peaks. The ideology and restrictions now being forced on the Faculty at Lake View are against many of my principles and philosophy. The unethical behavior demonstrated by Jerry Smith and David Green also might just be the tip of the iceberg. The dark side is gaining control."

"I will restart my clinical study protocol and basic research at the new Rocky Peaks Cancer Program. That Program will offer me the opportunity to become productive again and have more control over my own goals and future potential achievement. Phil Johnson has given me this chance, and I am going to take it."

"I cannot continue my clinical study protocol here because of this patient- code identity breech. I will stop enrollment today, and arrange to meet with each of the five patients already enrolled. These patients deserve to be told about the code identity problem. They need to know that due to the break in confidentially, the data obtained with their participation cannot be used in evaluating the effect of the Nanosphere Complex treatment. I will inform them of my decision to leave Lake View, and plans to restart the study in Colorado."

"I will tell these study patients that I have arranged with the Lake View finance department to pay for any remaining Nanosphere dose they have coming, if they want to continue and receive all three doses. The portion of my grant money that I leave with Lake View will also pay for follow-up laboratory and imaging studies as written in the approved protocol, if they want to stay with the study. Their clinical care will be continued with their own Oncology Physician."

"For those, if any, that remain in the study and the final three year follow-up, their data will be reviewed by myself and the NIH review panel. After that, I will then tell each patient as much as they care to hear about their own specific follow-up evaluation. I will explain to them the possible effects of the study on the progress of their bone metastases. They will understand that their data, of course, cannot be used with the data obtained from the patients that will be enrolled in the new Rocky Peaks protocol."

Wright interrupted Victor: "Will they be told which dose of Nanosphere Complex they received when you review their individual data at the three years conclusion?"

Victor said: "Yes Stan, I also owe that specific information at the time."

Victor then got up from his chair and extended his hand to Director Wright, saying: "So, Director Wright, thanks again for the support you have given me. I should be going now as I have several things to plan, act on and finish over the next several weeks. I hope we have another chance to talk together before I leave for Colorado."

Director Wright left his chair and firmly shook Victor's outstretched hand, saying: "Victor, it's been a pleasure knowing and working with you. I admire your professional productivity, your moral character and rational thinking. I respect your belief in the importance of liberty and oneself. I also know that the majority of your students and many of your peers also respect you for those characteristics. Please keep me in touch with your progress. I am hoping we meet again."

After thanking the Director for those comments, Victor Moritz left Director Wright's office.

- Epilogue-

It took six weeks for Dr. Moritz to finish at Lake View, including closing his clinical study. He talked with the five patients already enrolled, as he had discussed with Director Wright. All five patients decided to complete the three doses of Nanosphere Complex and remain committed to the follow-up lab and radiographic imaging studies for the required three years after entry. These patients realized that due to the patient dose – code identity breech, their progress and outcome of their bone cancer could not be used with any future data that Moritz might obtain from a new start of his protocol in Colorado. However, each wanted to be followed, whether improving or not. Then, after the three year follow-up, they wished to be told what progress there was, if any, and learn what dose of Nanosphere Complex they had received.

Moritz had an especially difficult time speaking with Jim and Rita about the unexpected sudden termination of the study. Jim, as usual, was supportive of Moritz's actions, and so was Rita. Jim was glad to stay in the study. Jim understood that if he lived for the next three years, he would know the results of his follow-up studies and the treatment dose group he was part of. Although Jim was unaware of the findings of the imaging studies so far, he actually felt that the intensity of his bone pain in his back and legs had decreased since he had entered the study several weeks ago. Although this was subjective on his part, he swore by his opinion as he told Moritz about it.

On parting, Jim and Victor had a good hand shake and a hug, and Victor and Rita a departing hug as well. Victor promised to keep in touch with them frequently. Unbeknown to Jim or Moritz at the time, Jim would be calling Moritz in nine months to say that his legs were virtually pain free, and he was starting to walk more each day.

***

Dr. Chen and Mark worked on packing the laboratory supplies and equipment that could be shipped to Colorado. Mark's dissertation was accepted by Lake View and he was awarded a PhD. in Biochemical Oncology. He joined Moritz and Chen in their laboratory at Rocky Peaks as a Postdoctoral Research Fellow. Dr. Li Chen was promoted to an Associate Scientist working in Moritz's lab. Charlie finished Medical School at Lake View and started his Residency at Northwestern University.

Moritz worked with the agencies that had awarded him grant money. He coordinated with the financial offices at Lake View and those at Rocky Peaks to be sure the transfer of the grant administration and amounts of the funding awarded to Moritz were accurate at both sites.

***

Victor had an emotional experience saying good-bye to his best friend and father figure, Otto Zellers. Otto was doing fine and fully recovered from the cardiac procedures he had undergone. He fortunately had not experienced the need for defibrillation, and the Pacemaker kept his heart rhythm steady, without Otto even being aware of its low intensity pulsing a few times a day. He was starting to drive his car short distances.

After hearing that Victor was leaving Lake View, Otto had talked with Amy about moving closer to her. She had located a single story small house for him that was in a neighborhood close to her family's home. He was putting his home in the Lake View area up for sale.

Victor had continued to drop in on Otto two times each week until moving to Colorado. They had good talks about their past, comparing childhoods of their different generations, medical practice experiences, parents, and more. They even shared their feelings of grief with losing their wives, which they had not spent any time sharing during the previous years they had known each other.

Otto agreed that Victor was absolutely right in leaving Lake View. He told Victor to continue his good work and seek the truth, not only in his science and medical pursuits, but in all he undertook.

Victor promised, on more than one occasion, to visit Otto at least once a year. Both were visibly moved during their final handshake on the day of Victor's departure. It was like they both knew, due to Otto's age, this visit might actually be their last together.

***

Six months after arriving at Rocky Peaks Cancer Program, Dr. Victor Moritz's clinical study of using the Nanosphere Complex for the treatment of prostate cancer bone metastases was entering patients at a rate of one new patient every week. Clinical care information, laboratory and imaging patient data were being securely collected at the required specific times, and regularly delivered to the monitoring panel at the NIH.

The Committee at Rocky Peaks that reviewed Moritz's clinical study, with NIH approval, required the addition of a placebo group to his protocol. Fifteen terminal patients with prostate cancer bone metastases would receive 3 courses of either Dose 1, Dose 2 of Dose 3 of Nanospheres that did not contain the attached Antibody Y on its surface, nor the anti-DNA compound in its core. They will receive the same follow-up studies as those receiving the 3 different Nanosphere Complex doses. There was some debate about the ethics of giving a group of terminal patients a placebo, which had also been considered by Moritz originally when at Lake View. However, the Committee at Rocky Peaks decided it would strengthen Moritz's study. These patients would be entered into study groups randomly and coded, just as all study patients were assigned to their respective groups.

Work in the laboratory by Moritz, Li, and Mark was moving forward. There was increased emphasis on the hypothesis of the possible role of the Nanosphere Complex in treating bone metastases from certain types of breast cancer. This was still dependent on basic animal model experiments, and the outcome of the present ongoing clinical protocol with prostate cancer bone metastases in humans.

Moritz's role in the lab was usually limited to reviewing new data with Mark and Li, and discussing future experiment possibilities. In addition, he was keeping up with the Nanosphere Complex clinical study protocol. Moritz was seeing and caring for an increasing number of his own new Oncology clinic patients. He was also enjoying his share of the teaching load as his academic commitment to the Department of Oncology. Friendships with Faculty peers and other Program staff were well on the way.

As promised by Phil Johnson, Moritz could decide on his own clinical patient load. His salary took into consideration the several years of experience and his expertise in the area of prostate cancer metastases. Also considered was patient satisfaction reports and his efficiency, yet sensitivity, in the clinic setting with elderly prostate cancer patients.

***

Ruth had left Phoenix and joined Victor at his apartment in Colorado two weeks after he had settled in. The apartment, dog friendly, was half a mile from the Rocky Peaks Cancer Program's location. During the next month, Ruth and Victor were married in a civil ceremony with Phil Johnson and Li Chen as witnesses.

Next came the purchase of a country home, surrounded by ten acres of trees and open land, in the foothills of the Rocky Mountains.
The view was awesome. Previous owners of the property already had a useable vegetable garden plot and a small well established mixture of shrubbery. The enclosed porch deck made a good place for Shadow's corner, and the fenced grounds gave him plenty of space to roam.

Ruth applied for and obtained a Nursing position on the Pediatric Oncology ward at Rocky Peaks. Her experience and interest in Nursing procedures had also led to a small, but fulfilling, role of doing some part-time teaching in the newly established Student Nursing rotation at the Rocky Peaks Cancer Program.

***

Some news from Lake View came from Director Wright on occasion. Several of those that Wright considered the best Faculty had resigned and left the Lake View Medical Center. Those leaving were not only from the Oncology Department, but other departments and support areas as well, such as the radiology and laboratory services.

It was becoming evident that David Green's Faculty Equity Committee's position and philosophy was increasingly supported by the President of Lake View. Although never finally proven, Director Wright had some information suggesting that Dr. David Green had been involved in getting the President to instruct his Administrative Assistant, Norma, to leak the patient-code data of Moritz's study. In addition, Green had never received any obvious reprimand for his actions with the Committee reviewing Moritz's study protocol. Even Jerry Smith was rehired after a temporary layoff.

Director Wright told Victor that he had accepted a position of Director of Medical Science at an Oncology program in Santa Fe, New Mexico. Dr. Rebecca Lopez, whom he was now dating, also left Lake View to work at that Oncology program in Santa Fe. They planned to join in marriage before the end of the year. He told Victor that Denver and Santa Fe were not too far apart, and maybe it would result in a chance for them to visit each other once in a while.

As the best left Lake View, referrals to the program declined. The remaining Faculty started cutting services and research for lack of research grant funds and operating capital. People in the area were wondering what was happening. In a few years, Lake View Medical Center closed.